M000072974

BIG DADDY
SINATRA
Carly's Cry

MALLORY MONROE

ISBN-13:978-0692652473 (Austin Brook Publishing)
ISBN-10:0692652477

AUSTIN BROOK PUBLISHING

This novel is a work of fiction. All characters are fictitious. Any similarities to anyone living or dead are completely accidental. The specific mention of known places or venues are not meant to be exact replicas of those places, but are purposely embellished or imagined for the story's sake.

VISIT
www.mallorymonroebooks.com
OR
www.austinbrookpublishing.com
for more information on all titles.

2

CHAPTER ONE

WHAT LOOKED LIKE CRAZY met Carly Sinatra as she entered the conference room at Reese Marketing. Her entire staff was there, six consultants in all, and all six were talking at once, answering phones, writing different ideas on the whiteboards all at once. They had so little continuity that it appeared as if they were six people handling six different cases. When, in truth, they were all handling the same case. The case of the former NFL quarterback.

Carly sat her briefcase on the table in the back of the room and then leaned her butt against the table. She watched her staff talk and write with each attempting to be the one to find the magic answer, when there was no such thing. But Carly let them do their thing. Her adopted father taught her the power of observation and she used it to stunning effect in her role as public relations director. That was why she didn't speak. She had to first see where they were coming from, she felt, before she could know where she needed to take them.

Upstairs, in what the employees called the Watch Tower, Trevor Reese and his client, former New England Patriots quarterback Ethan Campbell, were watching too. They were watching a series of closed-circuit monitors of Trevor's entire operation, but specifically of his conference room. His very chaotic conference room. And Ethan was not impressed.

"How are they going to help me, Trev?" he asked his long-time publicist. "They're as shocked as my fans are. And they're so young! How are these kids going to turn this around?"

Trevor, sitting behind the desk, calmly sipped more coffee, his large violet eyes dancing with mirth. "Carly will handle it," he said. "You just watch."

Ethan continued to stand behind Trevor's chair and watch the monitor, but he remained unimpressed. Those young Harvard hotshots never impressed him. Just a bunch of fast-talking *nerds* with zero common sense. And common sense was what he felt was needed. It didn't take a genius to know what he'd done and how much trouble he was in, and what he could possibly to do to beat the rap. It took a slickster. Carly Sinatra was a gorgeous girl with a smoking body, a body he had every intention of breaking one of these days. But in Ethan's eyes, there was nothing slick about her.

Trevor kept his eyes on Carly. Because he

knew her. He knew, as Carly sat in that conference room, she wasn't interested in being slick. She was interested in solving the problem. That was one of the reasons why he hired her. She was young, but she'd already amassed a reputation as one of the best crisis managers around. She was working out of California but wanted to return to the New England area where she once attended school when one of his head hunters told him about her, and he gladly snatched her up. And brought her to Boston.

And now seeing her with that innate patience, as her staff continued to chase their tails, made Trevor all the more certain of his choice. Because she never once made her presence known. It was her staff, after talking themselves into exhaustion and writing up all of the whiteboards, who finally bothered to look to her for answers.

"What are we going to do, boss?" one of her consultants asked. "We've come up with every conceivable option, and not one of them are viable. We could all lose our jobs if we don't get this right! You know how Mr. Reese can be! What are we going to do?"

"The first thing we will not do," Carly said calmly, "is panic. That we will not do." Then she exhaled and sat on the edge of the table.

"Tell me exactly what happened."

Most of them found such a request unnecessary. Surely she'd seen the morning news and read the morning newspapers? But they knew Carly. They knew it wasn't about whether or not she knew what happened, but whether or not she knew that *they* knew what happened. This was her way of getting their scattered minds back on the same page.

Murial Roadonsen spoke up. "Ethan Campbell was found in a hotel room with a girl he thought was twenty-one."

"But who turned out to be?" Carly asked.

"Thirteen," Murial said.

Carly felt an inward jolt. She even frowned. "How could anybody in their right mind confuse a thirteen year old for a full grown woman? Either he's dumb as dirt," she said, "or thinks we are. Which is it?"

Upstairs, Ethan heard her comment and ran his hands through his hair. "*Got*damn, Trev! She's worse than the media. I won't stand a chance with her running my PR!"

"She's making valid points," Ethan responded. "Just shut up and listen."

Ethan looked at Trevor with hate in his eyes. One day he was going to put that arrogant asshole in his place. But right now, he needed a powerhouse like Trevor on his side.

He therefore shut up, and continued to listen.

After some of the staff members gave their take on Ethan's motivation, with most judging Ethan guilty as sin in any event, Carly changed course. They were getting nowhere bashing the client. "Are there any photos?" she asked.

"Only what her family has released," Murial said. "There's been no trial. There hasn't even been an indictment. But already they're looking to sue the shit out of Ethan."

"Show me what we have," Carly said.

The projector came down, covering the whiteboards, and Murial grabbed the remote and pressed the button. The entire staff began commenting, shocked by the view.

When Carly saw the photos on screen, she wasn't as shocked as she was disheartened. Those photos were of innocence itself. Those photos were of a sweet, vibrant child who looked even younger than thirteen. And her heart began to pound. And decisively, yet unnoticed by everyone, her small hand began to slowly ball into a fist.

And she remembered every single one of those nights.

The hand over her mouth. That was always the first thing that flashed in her mind. Not the actual act, but the preparation for that act. His big, fat, clammy hand would cover her mouth.

She was usually asleep, or pretending to be, when he'd suddenly jolt her with the feel of his hand over her mouth. She would try to scream, but his hand was too big. Her little voice wasn't even muffled. His hand was so large, it went completely unheard.

Then he'd put on the duct tape. That was always next. That duct tape! She used to cry when the tape went on, tears would fall so hard that they would trace down her neck, until she realized no one heard her. She wasn't thirteen, like Ethan's victim, when it first started. She was nine. It all started just after Jenay and her father divorced. By the time she was thirteen, she was an old pro. By the time she was thirteen, there was no need for the tape because she stopped screaming and crying years before. Hundreds of years before. But he continued to cover her mouth, and tape it, anyway.

The best of those horrific nights was when it was just him. He'd lift up her gown, open her up, and ram it in. He came quickly, so it didn't last as long. He was small, so it didn't hurt as bad.

At least not the physical pain.

But most nights it wasn't him. It was the men who paid him. He got her ready. He covered her mouth and then taped her mouth.

He held her down while the men, one after the other one, all musky and sweaty and despicable, did her until she was bleeding. It was usually three a night. Sometimes four. Once she counted eight.

Each one would begin with a threat to kill her, and her sister, if she ever told a living soul. Then they would do her mercilessly, zip up their pants, and warn her all over again. Don't tell. Never tell. Some pointed guns at her, some pointed knives at her, some just pointed a finger. Then they'd pay and leave. She never knew how much they paid her father. But she saw them, after each encounter, pay him. And then her father would warn her too. With a gun to her head. Tell no one. Not even Ashley. *Not one living soul*.

While he lived, she couldn't tell. There were too many men. Too many warnings. Too much terror.

After he died, she wouldn't tell. There were too many memories of those men. Too many memories of those warnings. Too much *shame*.

Carly didn't realize she had completely shut down until the doors to the conference room opened, and Trevor Reese, their boss, walked in. His presence stopped her staff's accusatory conversation, and jolted her back in charge.

The tension in the room escalated as soon as he walked in. Not because he was a bad man that they all feared. It was because he was a powerful man they didn't really know. Carly had been in his employ for five months, and had assembled her entire team less than three months ago. For her staff, this was their biggest case yet. That was a source of the tension. The fact that Carly had already warned them that they would be summarily dismissed if they didn't produce results to the big man's liking and produce them fast, was the main source.

"Good morning, everyone," Trevor said in his familiar measured tone.

"Good morning, Mr. Reese," the staff said almost in unison.

"Good morning, sir," Carly said thereafter.

But Ethan had no time for niceties. He was already frowning and pointing. "What the fuck are those pictures doing up there?" he asked. "Take'em down! Take'em down right now!"

Carly's staff looked at her. She buttered their bread, not him. Carly, still calm as calm could be, Trevor noticed, nodded to Murial. "Turn it off," she said.

Murial quickly pressed the button and the screen went dark.

"That's better," Ethan said. "What the fuck

is wrong with you people? You work for me!"

"Actually they work for me," Trevor said, to the inward delight of the staff. "And speaking of work, Miss Sinatra," he added, to Carly. "What are we going to do about this little problem my client has?"

Carly looked at Ethan. He was the only man she'd ever worked for who never came onto her. He was the only man she'd ever worked for who had her complete respect. "We are going to do what we have to do," she responded.

"And that is what?" Trevor asked.

Carly didn't skip a beat. "Decimate her," she said.

Ethan smiled. "Well alright!"

Trevor, however, continued to stare, unabashedly, at Carly.

MALLORY MONROE

CHAPTER TWO

The jet black Mercedes-Maybach S600 turned onto the dirt road that led into a rough-looking neighborhood, and Jenay Sinatra looked up surprised. She had been studying contract proposals for the Bed and Breakfast she ran, and hadn't realized where Ashley had driven her. She leaned forward and looked out of the windshield at the neighborhood before them, at the dogs, the broken down cars, the dilapidated houses and trailers. Then she looked at her adopted daughter. "Where are you taking me?" she asked.

Ashley Sinatra smiled and jerked her long, weaved hair behind her back. "I just want to check on something."

"Ash," Jenay said like a woman who knew her well. "Check on what?"

"Nothing, Ma, come on. I need to see something."

"See what? And why in an area like this?"

"It's not as bad as it looks," she said. "It's just country back here, that's all. But this is where he says she lives."

"But are you sure this is the right street?

Maybe we're on the wrong street, Ash."

"Bobby said this is where he dropped him off. Bronson Avenue. At the blue house on the right hand side of the street, something like the eighth house from the corner, he said. I can only go by what he told me."

Jenay shook her head and leaned back. "Of all the girls in Jericho, of all the good, decent girls all around this town, leave it to Beaver to pick some biker chick from the hood. A biker chick that might even *wear* a hood!"

Ashley laughed, as the Mercedes drove past the fifth house on the opposite side of the street, a bungalow on the left hand side, and Kasper Coffman watched it drive past. It wasn't everyday a car like that turned onto Bronson, which was the main reason he bothered to look. But then again, he thought, it wasn't everyday Big Daddy Sinatra was standing on his front porch either.

He stared at Big Daddy as he read the note. "What's it saying?" Kasper asked him. "I come home from working a double shift and I find that orange piece of paper on my door. I know it's got something to do with the city because I can see the city logo there on it, but I don't know what it can be. I ain't got no dealings with this here town."

"Big Daddy" Charles Sinatra stood on

Kasper's porch and removed the sunglasses off of his narrow face, dangling them from his hand, as he read the note. Charles didn't have time for this. It was a workday, a very busy workday, and there were fifty other far more compelling business matters he needed to attend to. As the town's majority property owner, he was already stretched too thin. But Kasper was his long-time tenant, a hardworking man, poor all his life, who could barely read. On those rare occasions when he needed official documents explained, he called Charles. And Charles, loyal to those who were loyal to him, always came. "It's a notice of inspection, Kass," Charles said.

"An inspection?" Kasper asked, his fat, pink face turning red. "What inspection? I don't have nothing of theirs to inspect."

"It's the house," Charles said as he folded the notice and handed it back to Kasper. "They need to inspect the house."

Kasper looked at Charles with a wary eye. He respected Charles above any other man around town, but they were too different for him to fully trust him. Charles, for instance, was dressed in nothing fancy, just his usual professional attire: today it was a brown suit, white shirt, and brown tie, with a brown bowler hat on his head. But he stood in stark contrast to Kasper's oil-stained blue jeans and sweat-stained t-shirt, and the dusty porch they stood upon. But both men looked overworked and tired. Neither man wanted to deal with some notice from the city. "What business is theirs about this house? You got to explain that to me."

"There's apparently been some allegation of unsafe living conditions," Charles said to his tenant. "And they need to look into it."

"But what allegations?" Kasper asked. "What unsafe? What are they talking about, Big Daddy?"

It always felt odd to Charles when men older than he was, as Kasper clearly was, would call him *Daddy* anything. But that was his fate in Jericho. Everybody called him *Big Daddy* Sinatra as if they were sarcastically making his extensive property ownership synonymous with *Big Brother*. But because it wasn't an affectionate nickname, there was a time when they would only use it behind his back. But now, as the years of use and overuse made the term more and more common, and as the meaning became more and more obscured, they took to calling him the nickname to his face. It used to annoy the hell out of Charles. Now he didn't give a shit.

"I've been living here damn near ten

years," Kasper continued. "What they got to do with how I'm living? It's my business how I keep my house. What they got to do with it?"

Kasper could tell Charles was getting impatient with him, but he couldn't help it. He hated government overreach and he was certain that notice affirmed his distrust. He looked at Charles as Charles pushed the rim of his hat up a little, revealing more of his soft forehead against the beaming Jericho sun. Kasper wasn't a man given to bromances with other men or anything close to it, but he could easily see why the ladies loved Big Daddy. With his tanned skin and muscular body, and his full eyebrows and big, intense green eyes, Big Daddy was a very handsome man. But he was mean as a junkyard dog, and Kasper saw that side of him too.

"According to what they're saying there," Charles said to Kasper, "somebody apparently drove by the house, saw that it was loaded down with junk. And it is," Charles added as he looked around at all of the junk appliances and furniture on the front porch, and all of the junk cars around the yard. "And that person called in a report. To make sure it's not loaded with junk on the inside, the city is serving you notice that they're coming out within ten days to see inside for themselves. They want you to call that number at the bottom of the notice and schedule a time for them to come out. But it has to be within that ten day window, or they'll come without permission. They haven't rendered any judgment yet, but they will once they get out here."

But Kasper was still confused. "But what they got to do with anything? You own this house and I rent it from you. I've been renting this house from you for years. This is between you and me. What does any of it have to do with them?"

"They have to follow up on the complaint, Kass," Charles said. "They have to make sure your house is safe to live in. That's all this is about."

But Kasper continued to stare at Charles. Charles exhaled. He wasn't getting through to this man at all. So he stopped trying. "I wouldn't worry about it," he said. "The worse they can say is that it's messy around the place and you need to clean it up. Clean it up before they get here. If there's some repairs that need to be done, let me know. I'll have maintenance out here to handle it. It's nothing to worry about. Don't let it rob your peace."

"And if my idea of cleaning don't agree with their idea?" Kasper asked.

Charles frowned. "Then fuck'em," he said.

Kasper laughed. That was the Big Daddy he liked. But as he laughed he looked away from Charles and saw where the Mercedes had stopped in front of his neighbor's house some three doors down and across the street. Two African-American women got out of the car: one young, tall, and slender, and one older and slender, but easily more attractive than the younger one. "Speaking of fucking," Kasper said with a toothless grin, "I wouldn't mind a taste of those two black gals right there."

Charles knew Kasper was a vulgar man and dismissed his foolish talk. Kasper wasn't known as a dirty old man for nothing. But when Charles turned and saw the Mercedes that looked a lot like the Mercedes he had purchased for his wife, and then saw that those two *black gals* Kasper referred to belonged to his wife and adopted daughter, he did a double take. Not because Kasper was disrespecting his lady: he was relatively certain Kasper had no idea who he was married to. But because he had no idea why Jenay and Ashley would have any business in a neighborhood like this.

"Nicely packed those two," Kasper said. "But I'll take the shorter one, I think." But then Kasper turned his attention back to his own problems. "I have a confession to make, Big Daddy," he said. "A real big one."

Charles turned back toward his tenant. Was this confession related to his wife and daughter? "What is it?" he asked him.

"I don't know how to say this," Kasper confessed, "but I may be in trouble. Serious trouble."

Charles was especially curious now. "Yeah? Why?"

"The thing is, I don't exactly have what you would consider the cleanest house in Jericho."

Charles smiled. And then laughed. And turned his attention back to the matter at hand: that city notice. "Nobody does, Kass," he said.

"But why are they singling out my house anyhow?" Kasper wanted to know. "I'm a simple man, Big Daddy. All I do is work my hands to the bone. That's all I do. Work like a dog most every day. I don't have time to be bothering with no city officials. I don't have no fancy education like they have, or no big time job. But I pay my rent on time and I don't be bothering none of them. Why all of a sudden they're bothering me? Why all of a sudden they're talking about showing up here to do all of this inspecting? You own damn near half of the houses in this whole town, but I ain't never seen no city inspecting any of your other houses. But all of a sudden they're dying to inspect mine?"

While Charles attempted to explain the unfortunate prerogatives of city inspectors, Jenay and Ashley stood on the front porch of another house on Bronson Avenue. Only this house, if Robert was to be believed, was inhabited by Donald's latest girlfriend. And Donald had been dropped off there a few nights ago. Jenay was there because Donald, her youngest stepson who helped manage the Bed and Breakfast Charles put her in charge of, wasn't answering his cell phone and hadn't been to work in three days. She was worried about him. Ashley, Donald's best friend and adopted sister, was worried too. She knocked vigorously on the door.

As they waited for a response to the knocks, Ashley looked across the street, three doors down, and saw first a big Ford F-150 pickup truck that looked very much like her adopted father's. Then she looked further and saw her father standing on that porch in conversation with an older man. "Uh-oh," she said to Jenay. "There's Dad."

Jenay looked too, placing her hand over her forehead to shield the sun. When she saw Charles, she was astonished. "Goodness gracious," she said. "Does he own property on this street too?"

"Apparently," Ashley said.

Then Jenay exhaled. "Let's just hope he doesn't see us."

That didn't make sense to Ashley. She looked at her mother. "Why not? What's the big deal?"

"This neighborhood, that's what."

Ashley frowned, confused. And then she smiled. "Oh, I forgot," she said with a grin. "You're his queen. He doesn't allow his fragile queen to go anywhere near anything that isn't prime real estate. It's not a bad neighborhood, Ma, I told you."

But when the biker chick flung open the door, and all they could see were dark tats on her pale white skin, and biceps to rival Charles's, and an annoyed, angry face, they both saw the irrelevance of whether the neighborhood was bad: this woman didn't look to be about anything good.

"We're looking for Donnie," Ashley said as soon as the lady stepped out. She was average height, in her thirties, but was thick and solidly built. "Is he here?"

"And who are you supposed to be?" the woman asked. Then she frowned. "Are you her?" she asked. "You're that bitch?"

Jenay immediately touched Ashley on the arm. "Let's get out of here," she said, turning

22

to leave, certain she should have turned around in the first place when she saw where this house was located. This was a bad idea all around.

But the woman's singular focus was on Ashley. "You're his bitch," she said, as if it was a fact.

"I am not his girlfriend, if that's what you mean by bitch," Ashley made clear. "I'm his sister."

But the woman wasn't listening. "You're the one," she said. "You're that bitch he's been fooling around with. The one that works at the Tool and Dye."

Ashley frowned. "What?"

"I didn't believe it when they told me. But it's true. You're that bitch. And you have the nerve to come to my house? To *my* house?"

"Girl bye," Ashley said with great annoyance as she turned to leave too, holding her hand up in an obvious diss, but the woman grabbed her by her weave, pulling her backwards, and slammed her to the floor. Ashley screamed so loud that Kasper and Charles heard the scream and both looked in that direction. Jenay tried to pull the woman off of Ash, but the woman turned and put her free arm around Jenay's neck, pulling her to the floor right along with Ash.

"Get this fool," Jenay began yelling. "Lord, get this fool!"

When Charles saw that woman slam his wife onto that porch, his heart dropped through his shoe, his sunglasses dropped from his hand, and he took off running. Kasper was stunned. It was just a stupid cat fight for goodness sake. But nobody fought, cat or otherwise, with Charles Sinatra's wife. He ran across that street so fast he was up on the porch within seconds. And it was his time to do the slamming.

He grabbed that woman away from Jenay, which also got her away from Ashley, and flung her so forcefully that she nearly fell over the porch rail. Ashley was angry that the woman had messed up her two-hundred dollar hairdo, and was about get her revenge. Jenay didn't wear weave, but she was gearing up for a confrontation too. They felt blindsided when that woman came at them so aggressively. Now they wanted to blindside her.

But Charles shut it all down. As the woman moved to get back up, he held his arm around Jenay's narrow waist while pulling Ashley back too. "But she hit me!" Ashley was angrily crying, ready to fight back. "I'm not going to let her get away with jumping on me like that!"

Charles pushed her away. "Get in the car!"

he ordered her.

"But she hit me, Daddy!"

Charles looked at his daughter. He did not allow back talk, and every one of his children knew it. "What did I say to you?" he asked her.

Ashley and her baby sister Carly were adopted by Charles and Jenay into the Sinatra family, but even they knew their father would knock them through a wall if they disobeyed him. They knew he was not the one to trifle with. But Ashley's natural instinct wasn't to cower and go along to get along. She pushed boundaries. "You told me to get in the car," she admitted, "but what about the fact that she hit me, Dad? I can't let this Dollar General hoe get away with that!"

"Who are you calling a hoe, *hoe*?" the woman asked, and she and Ashley were about to go at it again.

Charles pulled Ashley back again, but this time he slung her down those steps so hard she fell onto the sidewalk. "Get your ass in that car, and get in there now!" he ordered her. Ashley, seeing the anger in his big, green eyes, got up and ran to the car.

Then Charles turned his attention to the combative woman. She moved back when she saw that she was no match for him too, and hurried toward her front door.

"Is Donald in there?" Jenay asked as the woman hurried past her.

"No, he ain't here, and you know it!" the woman decried. "Y'all just came here to start something!" she added, as she hurried into her house.

Charles grabbed Jenay by her elbow and pulled, all but dragged her off of the porch and down to the curb where her Mercedes was parked. Ashley was behind the wheel. She pressed down the passenger side window as they walked up.

"Take the car and go home," Charles ordered her. And then, realizing which child he was dealing with, added: "Go straight home or I'll kick your ass, Ashley!"

Jenay moved to get into the car too, since she and Ashley rode over there together, but Charles held her back. "You're coming with me," he said.

And as Ashley cranked up and drove away, to go straight home as he had ordered, rubbing her hair down as she drove, she was fuming at that woman. She was fuming at Donald for forcing her to have to look for his ass. She hit the steering wheel as she drove.

Charles pressed his hand hard against the small of his wife's back and walked her across the street, three doors down, to his truck in

Kasper's driveway.

Kasper was still standing at his front door as Charles placed Jenay on the passenger seat of his truck, walked around, and got in too. Kasper had heard how Big Daddy married himself a black woman, but he had no idea she would be the one. Not such a sweet, kind-looking woman like that. She didn't look mean and hateful at all. Kasper always assumed the woman who would become Charles's second wife had to be a little like his first one: mean and hateful too. But he didn't see that in this one at all.

What he also didn't see was Charles again. Charles left Kasper, and his sunglasses on Kasper's porch, backed out of the driveway and, without giving his tenant a second glance, sped away.

Charles kept glancing at Jenay as he drove, as if he was trying to decide if he even wanted to address what had just transpired. Jenay certainly didn't want to. She reached into his glove compartment, grabbed the comb she knew he kept inside, and combed her messy hair. Her hair was medium length, brown, and bouncy, and with the kind of layered cut that allowed her to comb it back, and then push it into a fluff-up that automatically settled into a reasonable style. Charles couldn't help but notice how gorgeous she looked when she fluffed it back up. He also noticed debris on the pants of her pantsuit, apparently acquired when she fell on that porch. When he stopped at a red light, he brushed it off of her. Then looked at her. "What the hell was that about, Jenay?" he asked.

"I was looking for Donald," she responded.

"You don't come down in this hellhole looking for anybody! If you need to find Donald you contact me, or Brent, or even Anthony or Robert. But what you don't do, and you'd better not do again, is get in a car with Ashley of all people and drive to this side of town. I nearly died when I saw that woman knock you down!"

Jenay looked at him. The tenor of his voice had changed.

"What if I hadn't been on that street, Jenay? What if I didn't hear your cry?"

"Stop worrying about me like that," Jenay said with a frown. "I would have been alright."

"Yeah, sure. That big-ass woman would have beat the shit out of you and Ashley both!"

"That's what you say," Jenay said. "But I would have handled my business."

The light turned green. Charles looked at her. "When we get home," he said, as he drove under the light, "I'm going to handle mine."

Jenay looked at him as he continued to drive. She knew what he was capable of. "What do you mean, Charlie?" she asked a husband who now seemed bound and determined to let his actions speak for him. And that determination was what was worrying her. "Charlie," she asked again, "what's that supposed to mean?"

CHAPTER THREE

"But things have changed," Donald Sinatra said to Tony and Robert, his two brothers, as they sat around the center island of their parents' kitchen, and he stood on the opposite side. The television on the kitchen wall was still on, showing a *Judge Judy* repeat, forcing him to speak a little louder than his usual voice. "We are a far cry from the way things used to be. I mean come on, man. We twice-elected the first black president of the United States. If that isn't progress, what is?"

"There's progress," Tony said, "but there's still racism too. Both can be true. I know this for a fact. I have a PhD in Clinical Psychology, remember? I have a syndicated radio therapy show, remember? I listen to that racist bull crap all day long. You should hear some of the nonsense people call into my show and proclaim. Some people still harbor those kind of views. And some of those people, I am sorry to say, are right here in Jericho."

"Yeah," Robert said, scrolling through his cell phone messages, his mouth cocked into a half smile, "like that biker chick Donnie's been fooling around with. What's her name?"

"Gilda," Donald said. "Gilda Lane."

"Yeah, her."

Donald looked at Robert. They were very close in age, but Robert acted as if he was as old as their oldest brother Brent. He sometimes came across to Donald as if he thought he was superior. "For your information, Mister Know-it-all," he said to him, "Gilda is not like that. You're just stereotyping. Just because she's a white woman with tats on her arms and who happens to enjoy riding a Harley every once in a while doesn't make her a racist, okay?"

Robert knew there was more to his belief than the fact that Gilda had tattoos and rode a Harley, but he wasn't going to argue with Donald about any of his females. He never listened to reason, Robert never listened to him, their arguments always went nowhere. Robert continued to scroll his messages.

"But why Gilda?" Tony asked Donald. "That is what I don't understand. You and Bobby are the blonds in the family. Both of you took after our mother. And both of you have the worse luck when it comes to women. I thought blonds had more fun?"

Robert grinned. "They do," he said with a raise of his eyebrows.

"And why wouldn't I like Gilda?" Donald asked. "She's good people. And who are you to talk anyway, Tony? She looks way better than those ugly barfs you always go for."

Robert laughed.

Before Tony could respond, the front door opened on the opposite end of the great room, and Ashley walked in. This was their new home that was built after a fire took out their old home, and everybody was still adjusting to the difference. Everybody was also adjusting to Ashley's appearance. "You look like Don King's sister," Tony said to her.

Ashley, however, gave Tony the hand and continued to stare at Donald.

"What's the matter with you?" Donald asked as she approached him. He and Ashley were best friends. "What happened to you?"

"Like really, Donnie?" Ashley asked as she stood beside him. "You're *here*?"

Donald was puzzled. "Where was I supposed to be?"

"Bobby said he dropped you off at crazy lady's house three days ago."

"And I did," Robert said.

"Stop calling her that," Donald said. "She's not crazy."

"She'd better be glad that's all I call her," Ashley said, "when I get through with her."

"I take it crazy lady is responsible for your new hairdo?" Tony asked.

"What happened?" Donald asked, looking at her disheveled hair.

But Ashley pushed him on his arm. "*Where were you*? We've been all over this town looking for you. Nobody heard from you for three days. You have Ma worried about you!"

"Perhaps you could have phoned him on his cell phone," Tony suggested.

"*Duh*," Ashley said. "That was the first thing we did, Genius. He wasn't answering his cell phone."

"Don't pay Tony and Bobby any mind," Donald said. "They think they're smart because they have book knowledge, when neither one of them have any common sense. They're just a couple of---"

"*Educated fools*," Donald and Ashley said together, and then high-fived. "So don't even give them a response to their foolish suggestions," Donald added.

"But where were you?" Ashley asked. "We went to your girlfriend's house on Bronson and she tried to beat me and Ma's ass."

Everybody was astounded. "She *what*?" Tony asked. "She put her hands on Jenay?"

"You're lying, Ash," Donald said.

"For real though," Ashley said. "Look at my

hair, if you don't believe me. She dragged me across her little front porch and knocked down Ma and tried to drag her too."

Tony stood erect. "Is Ma alright?" he asked.

"She's alright," Ashley said. "And so am I, Tone, even though I know you aren't going to ask."

"Gilda dragged Ma?" Donald asked, still astonished.

"She tried to," Ashley responded.

Even Robert had stopped strolling for messages on his cell phone and was listening too. "What's wrong with that lady?" he asked. "Wait till Dad hears about this. He won't beat a girl, but he's going to beat Gilda's ass when he finds out she touched Ma."

"Dad was there," Ashley said, and everybody looked at her. "He almost threw that woman off the porch getting her off of Ma. You should have seen him. He was red hot, you hear me? He told me to get my black ass back home, which I have done, and he's personally driving Ma home as I speak."

Tony looked at Ashley doubtfully. "Dad, our father, told you to get your *black* ass back home?" Tony had suspicion in his eyes. "Somehow I rather doubt Dad used that terminology."

"He didn't," Robert said, as he returned his attention back to his cell phone messages. "Ash is just being the drama queen as usual."

"Okay," Ashley admitted, "he didn't say black. But so what? He told me to get my ass back home. What's the difference?"

"There is no difference," Donald agreed. "But you see what I mean? They major in the minor things of life and still think they're so smart."

"You really have a complex about our intellect, little brother," Tony said. "You really ought to have that checked."

Robert grinned.

"You really ought to go play with yourself, big brother," Donald replied, and Ashley laughed.

"But for real though," Ashley then said to Donald. "Where were you?"

"I was with Gilda," Donald admitted. "At least I was until this morning when I was barely awake and she wanted some more. I couldn't take it anymore. My johnson couldn't take it anymore. That woman wears me out, I'm telling you!"

Ashley laughed, and so did Tony and Robert.

"I'm serious," Donald said seriously. "At first it was exciting. I could play hooky from work for a few days and just hang out with this nympho. This world class nympho. But that gets stale real quick when it's day in and day out all the time twenty-four-seven no time to breathe or shit or do anything else!"

They all laughed.

"I had to get my *white ass* away from there," Donald added.

Tony and Robert looked at each other and rolled their eyes. "Now he's channeling drama queen Ashley, of all people," Robert said. "What is this world coming to?"

Donald looked up when he heard a door slam outside and saw his father's big truck through the bay window across the room. Charles had gotten out and was walking toward the passenger side. "Dad just drove up," Donald said. Since he and Ashley were the only two standing on the opposite side of the island, she looked too. "With Mom," Donald added when Charles opened the passenger door and Jenay stepped out.

"Does he look angry?" Robert asked without bothering to look behind him.

Donald looked at his brother. "When does Dad not look angry?" he asked.

"When he's with one of his three favorite children," Tony said.

"Three?" Ashley asked. "What three? I

know Carly is his favorite, and little Bonita. But who's number three?"

Robert looked at her as if she had lost her mind. "Think, child. Think."

"Stop asking her to do something that is woefully unfamiliar to her," Tony responded.

"Ha ha, very funny," Ashley said. Then she realized who Donald meant. "Oh, Brent!" she said. "Yeah, right. Him too."

The front door opened, and Charles and Jenay walked in. When Jenay saw Donald, she broke from Charles and headed toward him. "Well good afternoon, Mr. Sinatra," she said to him.

"I was going to call you, Ma," Donald said, "but I forgot."

"You forgot that you're being paid, quite handsomely by your father I might add, to do a job? To show up for work when you're scheduled to be there?"

"I know," Donald said. "Sorry."

"Where were you?" Charles asked as he made his way to the kitchen area too.

"With crazy lady," Ashley said.

But then a TV commercial came on that mentioned their name by name. All of them looked toward the television screen.

"If you vote for me," said Herb Cruikshank, a tall politician at a campaign rally, "I will put an end to Sinatra domination in Jericho County once and for all!"

The rally crowd cheered vigorously.

"I'll kick that Brent Sinatra out of that same back door he walked in when he first became chief of police. He wasn't next in line for that job. Nowhere near it. But Big Daddy got him that job."

Tony couldn't believe it. "What a blatant lie," he said.

"And I won't stop there," Cruikshank continued. "I'll get rid of Makayla Sinatra too. Elect me and she'll be out as our District Attorney." The audience applauded wildly.

But Robert was confused. "He can't do that," he said. "Can he?"

But those with the answers, Charles, Jenay, and Tony, were still staring at the television.

"I'll kick her right out," Cruikshank continued. "Right along with her corrupt husband the chief. She's not a Jerichodian anyway. She's just some outsider nobody never heard of before she came to town. How did she get that job over all of those good men and women who'd spent years in the DA's office? Big Daddy rigged the system, that's how. He got her that job!"

"Lie after lie," Tony said. "Who would vote for such a person?"

But Cruikshank was feeding off of his very supportive, very conservative crowd. "You know what else I'll do when I'm elected?" Cruikshank asked. "I'll end the stranglehold Big Daddy Sinatra has had on our community once and forever more. Vote for me," Cruikshank said, "I'll set you free! I'll get rid of Big Daddy's influence in the county once and for all!" The crowd went wild. Tony grabbed the remote and turned off the TV. "That kind of slander, my fellow Americans, is bad for your health."

"But he can't kick Brent out of his job," Ashley said. "Can he?"

"If he wins the election, he can," Tony said. "Brent was appointed chief by the mayor and serves at the pleasure of the mayor. If Cruikshank becomes mayor, he can fire Brent."

"But he can't get rid of Makayla. She was elected DA. He can't change that."

"They already have," Tony said. "The city council voted last year to place the office of the DA under the mayor's jurisdiction. No more elections for DA. The mayor gets to appoint that post now."

"They can't legally do that," Robert said, "but it'll take a lawsuit to get them to back down."

"Dad, you hear that?" Donald asked. "Cruikshank wants to fire Brent and Makayla."

"Speaking of firing," Jenay said to Donald. "Your lame excuse that you *meant to call* your job, is unacceptable. You're fired."

Donald was shocked. "Fired? What did I do?"

"You have not shown up for work for three straight days, Donald. You would not answer your cell phone, I had no clue where you were. And we had emergency after emergency at the Inn. I didn't hire you as my GM for your health!"

"And you even removed any ability we had to track you," Ashley added. "That's why I drove over to crazy lady house."

"But you're firing me?" Donald asked his stepmother. He was still reeling.

"Yes, I'm firing you," Jenay said. "What did you think was going to happen? You wouldn't pull that stunt on anybody else's job, but you think you can pull it on me because your father owns the hotel? I have a zero tolerance policy at the Jericho Inn and you know it. We're looking to expand. We're looking to become, not just the best in Jericho, but the best in Maine. I need a reliable general manager."

"I am reliable! I work my butt off. You don't know what the hell you're talking about!"

Charles reached over and slapped Donald hard across the face, causing Donald's blond hair to sling from the right side of his face to the left side. "Say it again," he prodded him.

Donald grabbed the side of his face. "I didn't mean it like that," he insisted.

"Then don't say it like that," Charles insisted. "Jenay is not only your stepmother, she's your boss. And you will respect her in both roles. You understand?"

Donald, growing red with anger, didn't respond to his father. Charles began to move from beside Jenay and closer to Donald.

Donald winced at the thought of another hit. "I understand," he said quickly. He looked at Jenay. "Ma, I'm sorry," he said. "I should have phoned."

"What you should have done was show up for work," Jenay said.

Robert grinned. "You wouldn't believe what he was doing while he was away," he said.

"Shut up," Ashley said, defending Donald as she usually did. "You're just trying to make it worse."

But Charles looked at Ashley. "You already attempted that," he said to her.

"I didn't do anything to make that woman jump on Ma," said Ashley. "I just asked her if Donnie was there. She was the one who assumed I was his girlfriend."

But Charles wasn't buying it. "The next time you fix it in your brain to go to a place like that to look for somebody," he said, "you take Tony or Robert or even Brent. But you do not take my wife. Do you understand me?"

Ashley swallowed hard. She saw what Big Daddy did to Donald. "Yes, sir," she said.

"Your father is under a tremendous amount of stress with all of this talk of the city invoking eminent domain and taking over his properties," Jenay said. "That's what Cruikshank is talking about, and he and that crooked city council can conspire and do just what he's saying. We all need to keep it together. He doesn't need these side shows."

All four children looked at their father. They knew the campaign rhetoric was taking a toll on him. But they thought it was just talk. They never thought, not once, that it could actually become a reality.

"The last thing he needs is for you guys to add to his stress," Jenay added.

Charles looked at Jenay as if he couldn't believe her nerve. "And you think you haven't added to my stress?" he asked her.

"Me?" Jenay asked, surprised he would even suggest it.

"Yes, you," he said, surprised she wouldn't understand it. And then took her hand and began leaving with her. "You come with me. We have unfinished business," he added, as he escorted her up the side stairs.

When they were out of earshot, Ashley looked angrily at Donald. "See what you've done?" she said. "Now Dad's going to get on her case because of your stupidity."

"I said I was sorry!" Donald responded. "I'm not the one telling him to get on her case about it."

But Tony was shaking his head. "Dad is going to get on her alright," he said. "But not like you mean."

Donald looked at him with a frown on his face. "Fucking at a time like this?" he asked.

They all looked at Donald. "A time like what?" Ashley asked him.

"People get tired of that," Donald said.

"If I had it twenty-four-seven like you were having it," Robert said, "I'd be tired too. But the rest of us don't live on planet Donald. We live on planet Earth. And on planet Earth, it is always a good time to fuck."

Even Tony, who eschewed vulgar language, smiled at that.

CHAPTER FOUR

Trevor Reese and Carly stood outside the press room as Trevor fielded a last minute phone call from one of his investigators. Carly stared at the man with the long, wavy hair and the gorgeous violet eyes. He had the kind of rock hard body most women would be glad to get to know. Including Carly. But that was strictly between her and her dreams.

When he finally ended the call, she moved closer to the door. "Ready, sir?" she asked.

They were already late for the press conference. Ethan Campbell was waiting in the press room, along with his dream team of lawyers. But Trevor was the spokesman. Trevor was the one they were waiting on. Yet he lingered in the hall. "What about you?" he responded. "Are you ready?"

Carly always found him to be an odd man. He was flashy in the clothes he wore and the cars he drove. And his good looks made him a female magnet even in her office. But he never took the bait. She'd never seen him with a lady on his arms- nor a guy for that matter, and he never came on to her or anybody else in his vast organization. She knew this to be true because the ladies complained about it endlessly, as if a man who looked like him and dressed like him had to be a whore. Why wasn't he whoring around on them? Even Carly had a secret crush on him when she first started working for him. But Trevor Reese kept it professional up and down the line. So professional that she began to feel guilty for even thinking such a thing. And she woke up from her dreams of being with a great guy like him, and kept it professional too. "I'm ready," she said. "I'm ready to get it over with."

"Then we shall," he responded, looking down her body and then back up to her face. But the way Trevor looked at her always seemed as if he was assessing, not her attractiveness as most men did, but her sense of style. As if he wanted to make sure her clothes were on point before they went into the room. He smiled when he looked back into her face, as if she passed the test. Then his smile quickly faded. "Let the disgust begin," he said with a flash of sadness in his eyes, eyes that were so blue they were violet, and opened the press room doors.

Carly was taken aback by the way he phrased what they were about to do. But no truer words could have been spoken. They were public relations people whose job was to keep their client as innocent as possible in the public eye. No matter what evidence said otherwise. No matter how disgusting that client truly was. This was what they did.

Trevor stepped aside and allowed Carly to walk in first, and they walked into the packed pressroom as if they were bearers of great news and the media was going to eat it up. Trevor walked up to the podium, while Carly took her place beside Ethan Campbell and his attorneys. They were all smiling because Carly, as PR point person, told them to smile. Smiling, she said, would minimize the seriousness of the allegations. As if they all had a secret, and that secret involved Ethan's innocence. Ethan, especially, had the grandest smile of all.

Trevor, however, wasn't given to anybody telling him what to do. This was nasty business and he wasn't going to pretend otherwise. He remained stoic as he stood there. He remained all-business as he presented the public case of Ethan Campbell.

"My client did not, nor could he have raped that young lady. They went out partying. They went out drinking. And it was all good to Ethan because she was twenty-one years old. Her ID said she was twenty-one. Her appearance said she was twenty-one. He had no reason whatsoever to suspect otherwise."

Then Trevor nodded to his computer guy, a nod that alerted him to get ready. "The picture the family is circulating to the media is this photograph."

The screen in the room showed a big picture of an innocent-looking thirteen-year-old.

"If that was the image that Amber Schwartz portrayed the night in question, then I, too, would be outraged. I, too, would recommend the harshest punishment for Ethan Campbell."

Ethan's smile almost left his face, but Carly moved closer to him, reminding him by her presence alone to keep up appearances. He continued to smile.

"But that wasn't the image she portrayed that night," Trevor continued.

The screen showed a series of photographs, of a much older looking Amber Schwartz in very suggestive clothing. The media snapped pictures of the images vigorously.

"This is the image Amber Schwartz portrayed the night Ethan met her," Trevor said. "And as you can see, she looks nothing like those photographs of an innocent thirteen-year-old the public has been inundated with. Amber Schwartz looks as if she is thirty, not thirteen."

Trevor began to describe the various photos. "There she is in yet another club," he said as a picture of her dancing in a nightclub came on screen. "There she is drinking with much older women. And men, by the way. And here she is showing off an ID that puts her age at twenty-one. An ID that looks completely real, folks."

Then he stopped looking at the photographs and turned his full attention back to the assembled media. "What in the world, I ask you, was Ethan supposed to do? What more, I ask you, could Ethan have done? And as to her rape charge? Give me a break! You don't party with a girl. Drink all night with a girl. And then, when the girl begs you to take her home with you, you take her home and rape her? She begged for it, and we have plenty of witnesses willing to make it clear that she begged for it. She begged for him to get it, but then he had to take it? Give me a break! He didn't rape anybody. He doesn't have a violent bone in his body. This woman, and I call her that because that is how she presented herself, is out for blood. Blood money. Pure and simple. Ethan Campbell is the real innocent in all of this."

Ethan's smile went into overdrive. He looked at Carly, pleased with the strategy she came up with. Decimate the girl, Carly had suggested, and that was exactly what they were doing. Carly was smiling too, and even returned Ethan's look with an even grander smile of her own. But it was all for the cameras. It was all for show. She was dying inside.

The knocks on her door later that night didn't make her feel any better. Especially when she opened the door quickly, certain it was her assistant Muriel. Muriel had just left her home a few minutes ago, and she thought she had forgotten something and had come back. She always forgot to mention something, or forgot something outright.

"What is it this time?" Carly asked cheerfully when she opened the door. When she saw that it was Ethan Campbell, she was stunned. But not so thrown that she couldn't move to quickly close the door she had just so casually opened. But his shoe blocked the way.

"What do you want?" she asked him.

"I just want to thank you," he said, that same fake smile she coached him to display on full display tonight, as he stepped into her home.

"There's no need to thank me," Carly said, folding her arms. "Step back out please."

But he closed the door instead. "Come on, now, Carly. You had a great strategy. And it worked! The least I can do is thank you. You came through for me. And you know why, right? Because you saw it too. That girl was no kid! You saw how quickly the DA dropped those charges. You saw how quickly he threw it all out. That's because of you. He saw right through that girl and her lies just like you did."

"I was only doing my job," Carly made clear. "I didn't see through anybody."

"Yes, you did," Ethan said with a grin. "You know you did. Because you know what it's like to have men wanting you, and lusting after you." He looked down her body. "Don't you?"

Carly's heart began to pound.

"I was driving by this area," Ethan continued, "and decided to drop by and see you. On the spur of the moment like. You know why? To thank you, yes. But you know my real reason?"

"I need you to leave. I'm not interested in knowing your real reason."

"My real reason for dropping by like this is because I know you," Ethan said, disregarding her request. "I know a hoe when I see one.

And you're one. You may fool Trevor and all of those other people in his office, but you don't fool me. It takes a hoe to know a hoe. I know you."

Carly's discomfort level shot through the roof. She unfolded her arms. "Leave my house at once," she said. "I'm not playing with you, Mr. Campbell!"

"Mr. Campbell," Ethan said with another grin. "I like that. You love to play the role of Miss Prim and Proper, don't you? But I know better." He placed his hand on her chin. "You like to fuck, don't you?"

She slapped his hand away. "Okay, that's it," she said, reopening the door. "Get out and get out now!"

But Ethan slammed the door back shut just as forcefully as she had opened it. "I'm not ready to leave. I'm not ready to get out now. How about that, Miss Proper?"

"Then fine," Carly said, heading for her cell phone on her coffee table. "We'll let the police handle it."

But before Carly could turn again, Ethan was upon her and violently knocked the phone out of her hand. Then he knocked her down with even more force. "The police ain't handling shit, bitch!" he said. And he said it with the kind of anger and bitterness that the public never saw. He said it with clenched teeth. And all of the smiling and charm he had laid on thick at that press conference, every ounce of it, was gone.

CHAPTER FIVE

They were in bed, and Jenay was on top. Charles still hadn't told her how she added to his stress because he was too busy sucking her breasts. And it was never a quick-off with Charles. He feasted on her breasts. His mouth did the sucking, his hand did the squeezing and rubbing, and all Jenay could do was feed them to him as if they were as good as food. They were going to be sore when he finished, she knew, but right now they could not possibly feel any better.

Charles loved sucking her nipples. He loved squeezing and fondling her big, brown mounds. He loved moving from breast to breast until they were red from his abuse. He didn't want to stop. He could suck her all night. But when she began turning red, which meant he was overdoing it, he knew he had to stop.

But Jenay knew his idea of stopping meant that he was stopping in that area of her body, and moving another area. That was why, when he moved her onto her back, and slid down between her legs, she knew more mouth action was coming. And it came. Charles began licking between her legs vigorously. He was craving her taste, and her breasts only gave him a sample. It was her pussy, it was the taste of her vaginal juices that wet her as quickly as his mouth dried her, that he was after. And he stayed after it for a long time. Jenay was squeezing the sheets, and he was lifting her thighs for greater access, until she was on the verge of an orgasm.

Charles wanted more. Her taste intoxicated him and he wanted to eat her as long as his mouth could chew. But he knew his wife. If she came now, it would be nice and she would enjoy it. But nothing like the orgasms she displayed whenever his cock took her over.

"Turn over," he said when he stopped giving her head, and she quickly turned onto her stomach. He leaned down, kissed her cheeks, licked her, and then put it in her. From the back. He pushed in and almost out, going further in with every push-in, until he was in his rhythm.

And he found his stroke as he kept hitting her special spot. He laid down on top of her bare ass, squeezed her tight beneath him, and fucked her like she'd never been fucked before. That was the way Charles always made her feel. As if this was their very first time. As if he was so in awe of her super-wet pussy that he was determined to dry it out. Only to wet it even more. Only to fuck her so hard that the sound of his pre-cum and her vaginal juices mixed together and created a harmony. They were in sync. And both of them were on the verge.

They rarely came together, but they came together this time. Charles was just feeling the squeeze against his rod, and Jenay was just feeling the pulsations within her folds, when they went over. He continued to fuck her, without letting up, as their harmony created rolls of white cream that saturated his penis, and her vagina, until there was nowhere for it to go but out. An overflow of cream slid down Jenay's thighs, as Charles still continued to fuck her. He was pounding, not only her pussy, but her ass too, as they fucked.

Jenay was holding onto the headboard, her upper body lifted slightly, as Charles put on her the kind of sex her fondest dreams were made of. She came again. And again. Until he was out of gas. Until he couldn't make another move. Until there were no more strokes left in him. He collapsed on top of her, their bodies filled with sweat and drain, and she collapsed too.

After several moments of heavy breathing and relaxation, Jenay was the first to speak. "And you had the nerve to say I stress you out," she said, in a voice barely discernible. She was still out of breath.

"Your pussy notwithstanding," Charles said, virtually out of breath too, "you do."

Jenay smiled.

"But it was great, my darling," Charles said, kissing her sweaty back.

"Yeah, it was," Jenay agreed. "But I'll pay the price. I'm going to be a sore motherfucker in the morning."

Charles laughed. "But don't you worry," he said, holding her even tighter. "I'll be thinking about you, and how you gave it to me in that magical way once again, every step of the way."

Jenay snorted. "I'll be sore, but you'll be thinking about me?" She smiled. "Some comfort you are!"

She fought like hell, but it felt like she was beating steel. She tried to scream, but he covered her mouth. When he lifted her and carried her to the bedroom, it felt as if she was floating in space. When he threw her onto the bed, he got on top of her and covered her mouth again. The feeling of his weight on her small body took her breath away.

"Scream, bitch," he said to her, again with clenched teeth, "and I'll kill you."

The murderous look in his small, blue eyes made her know this was nothing new to him. And the way he was doing her, the way he was stripping off her blouse and tearing off her bra, was just like the way that thirteen year old said he did her. The girl said, when he threatened her and ripped off her shirt, that she knew she had to give him what he wanted or he would kill her. And as he sucked Carly's bare breasts, she, too, felt like giving up. She felt like giving him what he wanted too. He was too big. She couldn't even breathe beneath his big, sweaty body.

But his hand wouldn't let her give up. Because his hand was covering her mouth. And it did something to Carly. That hand over her mouth felt like the same old thing coming back again. It felt like her father's hand. It felt like the same thing! She couldn't fight back then. She didn't know what fighting off a man meant back then. But she knew now.

She stopped hitting his back with her fists. That was a waste of energy. But she began looking for whatever advantage she could find. Because she didn't know how the evening was going to end, but she knew he wasn't raping her. She wasn't going to let him do to her what all those hundreds of men did to her and got away with it. She couldn't let him get away too.

All she had was her laptop on her bed, and as he attempted to suck her breasts dry, as he pulled down and completely removed her pants and panties while he sucked, rendering him sufficiently distracted, she grabbed it. She grabbed that laptop and slammed the sharp edge into the side of his head with such force that it knocked him off of her and caused him to start bleeding immediately.

But she didn't stop there. As soon as he got off of her, she jumped out of that bed and ran. When Ethan felt the side of his head and saw that there was blood on his hands, his anger heightened, and he got up and ran after her.

She ran down the hall, through the living room and into her kitchen. He ran down the hall, through the living room, and into her kitchen too. Only when he came in, ready to kill that bitch, he didn't see her at all. Was she already gone? Did she run through the backdoor in the kitchen? Had she gotten away from him?

He began to hurry toward the kitchen door in panic, to stop her if she got that far, knowing his freedom was on the line if she got away. It was one thing when a kid with no power accused him of rape. It was another thing when a sophisticate like Carly Sinatra did the same. No amount of PR was going to beat that rap for him!

But as he began moving toward the back of the kitchen, Carly, hiding behind the center island in the middle of the room, stood up with knife in hand and ran up behind him. Just as he was about to turn around, just as he was about to grab what his instinct told him was just behind him, she stabbed him in the back.

She was amazed that she had done such a thing. She was amazed at the force of her stab. And when he turned and looked at her, stunned that she would go that far, fear took her shock away. Because he didn't fall. Because he was about to take that knife from her and use it far more effectively than she had.

And that was why she knew she couldn't let up. She saw too much. She saw life going backwards to all those nights in that bedroom, and all of that helplessness. She stabbed him in the front. Straight through the heart. And she stabbed and stabbed and stabbed. He was down, as lifeless as an ornament, and she kept stabbing. She stabbed for her innocence lost.

She stabbed for her inability to trust. She stabbed for her inability to be anything but a bitch because her father and those men treated her as if that was all she'd ever be. And she stabbed.

When she finally came to herself, and saw the blood in her kitchen, and realized what she was doing, she stood up, and backed away from him. What had she done? *What had she done*?

She looked around, on the verge of sheer panic. She looked at the knife still dripping with Ethan Campbell's blood. And she ran. She ran to the living room to retrieve her cellphone. But it was busted. When Ethan knocked it from her hand so violently, it broke apart. Then she remembered her landline, the only one she had in the house, and ran back into her kitchen. Ethan was still there. Still lifeless. Still, she thought with horror deep within her soul, dead.

She grabbed the phone from its cradle on the wall and dialed direct. Not to the police, but to the only man she ever trusted in her life. She slid down the wall until her bare butt was touching the cold floor. And she put in a call to Big Daddy.

CHAPTER SIX

Brent Sinatra drove his father's Jaguar, with Charles on the passenger seat and Jenay in back, as they left Maine in a blaze of speed. They left as soon as the call came in. They drove nonstop to Boston, some two hours from Jericho, and pulled into the driveway of Carly's beautiful home on the lake in even less time. Charles's heart was pounding. He had a close relationship with all of his children, but his relationship with Carly, his adopted daughter, was what even he would describe as special. She was his golden child, and all of his children knew it. She was the only one of his grown children who never disappointed him. She made it with her brains and talent and she made it big. And for her to have this happen to her just broke his heart. He couldn't wait to get to her!

He was the first to jump out of the car and hurry to her front door. Jenay wasn't far behind him, and Brent wasn't far behind them. All three were worried sick. All three still couldn't believe the words Carly had spoken.

"I'm in trouble, Daddy," she'd said when

she phoned him. "I killed Ethan."

Charles didn't know who Ethan was, and he didn't care. He told her he was on his way. He and Jenay took Bonita to Brent's house for Brent's wife Makayla to take care of, and they, with Brent, took off. It was a two-hour drive, but they reached her home in almost half that time.

Charles, who visited her in Boston more than anybody else in the family, had a key to her home and did not bother to knock. He unlocked her door and hurried inside, with Jenay and Brent behind him.

"Car?" he yelled. "Carly?"

He ran through her house until he ran into the kitchen. And that was when he saw her. Her bare butt still sitting on that cold floor. Her torn blouse and bra. That blood-stained knife still in her hand. She didn't even bother to look at her father. She was still staring at Ethan.

Jenay's heart dropped through her shoe when she saw the dead man on that kitchen floor. And when she saw her baby, when she saw the child who was once her stepdaughter when she was married to Carly's father Quince, sitting in an almost catatonic state with that bloody knife in her hand, she pushed past Charles and made her way to Carly. She got on the floor beside her, and pulled her into her arms. But Carly continued to stare at Ethan.

Charles and Brent went over to the body and knelt down. Brent, the chief of police in Jericho County, checked to see if the man still had a pulse. The blood made it obvious that he did not, but in his line of work he never took anything for granted. He checked. Ethan Campbell's death was confirmed.

"I'll be damned," Brent said when he finally took a good look at the dead man. "I know him."

Charles, still knelt down with his expensive shoes within mere inches of the pool of blood, looked at his oldest child. "You know him?"

"Not personally. I know of him. That's Ethan Campbell, Dad."

Charles frowned. "Who's Ethan Campbell?"

"He used to be the quarterback for the Patriots."

"A starter?"

"He was the starter a couple of seasons. He once even made it to the Pro Bowl. He's a big deal."

Charles didn't want to hear that. Because the bigger the decedent, the worst it would be for Carly. He stood up. And then went over to Carly and knelt beside her and Jenay. He removed the knife from Carly's hand.

Jenay still held their daughter in her arms, but Carly continued to stare at the dead body. "Carly," Charles said, but she didn't even blink.

Charles and Jenay exchanged a glance. Jenay shook her head in agony.

Charles, his face frowned with anguish too, took Carly by the chin and turned her small, beautiful face toward his. "Carly," he said again. "This is your father talking. I need you to hear me."

And she blinked. When she realized it was Charles, when she realized it was Jenay, she blinked. And the tears began to flow.

As Jenay pulled her closer, to comfort her, Charles knew he had to hear the story. He had to know what he was going to do about this. "What happened, sweetheart?" he asked her.

It took her several moments, but then she was able to speak. "He tried to rape me," she said in that clear way she always spoke. She looked at Ethan again. "I wouldn't let him."

Charles nodded. "Good. You did the right thing."

Her voice sounded confident, but her face told a different story. "I killed him, Daddy. I stabbed him over and over and over again. I killed him." Then she looked at her father again. "Will they believe me?"

She asked a direct question because she

knew, with Charles, she would get a direct answer. He never bullshitted any of his children. That was why every one of his children respected him above any human being alive. "No," he said to her. "They will not believe you."

The tears streamed harder when he said those words, Carly's already distressed face turned even more anguished, and she placed her face in her hands. She began to sob. Jenay held her, and looked at Charles.

Charles fought back tears as he saw his daughter in anguish. And he knew he couldn't let it be. He touched her on the arm. She looked at him. "Don't worry, baby," he said to her. "They don't have to believe you. Nothing is going to happen to you. I promise you that."

Then Charles took the landline phone that was still off the hook, the landline phone that was beside Carly on the floor, and stood up.

But Brent hurried over, and placed his hand on the phone. "What are you going to do, Dad?" he asked. He knew his father.

Charles looked at Brent. "The only thing I can do."

But Jenay wasn't onboard. "Charles, you can't," she said. She feared for Carly, but she feared for her husband too.

"What do you mean I can't?" Charles

asked. "I have to, Jenay. Somebody's got to pay for this. You can't kill a man and there be no retribution. I have to handle this."

"But this is Boston, Charles." Jenay once lived in Boston for many years. "This isn't Jericho. Brent isn't the police chief here, and Makayla isn't the DA."

"She's right," Brent echoed. "You'll never see the light of day again if you take the fall for this."

"And what do you think Carly will see?" Charles asked him. "You think they'll go easier on my child? A young, black woman who killed their white hero? This superstar quarterback even you've heard of? They'll crucify her! She'll never see the light of day and she's still a baby!"

Brent, outdone, looked at Jenay. He knew, when his father was this high strung, only Jenay could talk him down. Tears began to drop from Jenay's eyes as she removed her arms from Carly, and stood in front of her husband.

That was the worse pain of it all for Charles. The fact that he might never see Jenay again. Or Bonita. Or the rest of his children. The fact that Jenay, by virtue of loving him so much, would be imprisoned too.

Jenay placed her hands on either side of his handsome face, and they touched forehead to forehead. She was in pain too, but she was not going to let it overtake her. They had to be practical. They had to see this for what it was. She stared into her husband's eyes. "I know you, Charlie. And you're a good man. You're the best father our children could have ever hoped for. But you cannot take the blame for this. None of us can bear this. Especially not Carly. And not you either."

Brent was relieved that Jenay was there. She was first and last a level head in their family.

"Then what is the answer, Jenay?" Charles asked her. She was his best counselor. "What are we going to do? If anybody in this room takes the blame, it has to be me. I protect my family." Emotion welled up inside of Charles as his voice broke. "Carly's my baby. From the moment that social worker said we could take her and Ashley with us, she's been my baby. She killed him in self-defense, but they won't believe her. Not with this many stab wounds." He looked at Ethan's body. Then he looked at Jenay. "What are we going to do?"

Jenay pulled the big man into her small arms. She didn't know what to do either.

But Brent, the lawman, did. "We've got to move the body," he said.

Charles and Jenay stopped embracing and

looked at him. The idea of straight-lace Brent suggesting something illegal on its face astounded them. But what he was suggesting astounded Charles more. "Move the body?" he asked with a frown on his face. "What are you talking about move the body?"

"We've got to get this body to Jericho," Brent explained. "I'm chief of police there, and my wife is the District Attorney. Jenay is right. We can have some control there. We don't have shit here."

"If Cruikshank wins that election," Charles said, "you won't have shit there either."

"They're trying to get rid of us," Brent admitted. "And if Cruikshank wins, they will get rid of us. But not before we refuse to prosecute you. Not before we declare it a case of self-defense and refuse to press charges."

Charles stared at his son. It was the first sign of hope they had. And right now, they were all grappling at straws. But the logistics of the thing! "How the hell are we going to move a body?" Charles asked, giving voice to his skepticism. "We don't know anything about moving a body."

Then Jenay's look suddenly changed. "But Mick does," she said.

Charles and Brent, both taken aback, looked at her.

She looked at Charles. "Mick does," she said again, with even more conviction, as if she was just beginning to believe it herself.

CHAPTER SEVEN

Mick Sinatra was in bed, on his back, fucking his wife. He was finally back home after an unproductive business trip that lasted a week longer than he had planned, and he missed his family terribly. Especially Rosalind. And he was bound and determined to show her just how much. They made love earlier, when he first hit town. But that was three hours ago. He wanted some again.

"*Rosalind*," he kept saying as he held her naked body tightly in his arms and pumped his ass off. She was on top, their bodies were pouring with sweat from the aggressiveness of their lovemaking, and Mick began rubbing his hands down her back and ass as the feelings intensified.

Rosalind could feel it too. She could feel his cock pound into her with such force and thickness that she felt as if her entire insides were inflamed. She was having orgasm after orgasm with every glide he made. She was lying on top of him, holding him as tightly as he was holding her, and all she could do was bite her lower lip, close her eyes, and enjoy the pound her man was putting on her.

When Mick's cell phone began ringing, they both were inclined to ignore it. Mick was on the verge of cumming, and Rosalind was already there. They would have ignored it had it not been for the distinctiveness of the ring. Mick designed that ring for only two people in this world: Rosalind, his beautiful African-American wife, and his big brother Charles.

He could not ignore Charles.

But that didn't mean he liked it. "Shit!" he said angrily when he knew he had to answer the call. But he still couldn't pull away from Roz. Her pussy had that magical flavor to him, and he was too hungry for it. He answered the phone, still pounding her. "What?" he asked, unable to shield his displeasure.

"Sorry to disturb you, Mick," Charles said over the phone, "but there's trouble."

Mick's strokes slowed. Rosalind was still too consumed in her own orgasms to notice right away. But Mick knew his brother. He did not toss words around for dramatic effect. If he said there was trouble, it was major. "What kind of trouble?" Mick asked.

"A man is dead," Charles said. "That kind of trouble."

Mick stopped stroking Rosalind so abruptly that she couldn't help but notice this time. She lifted her head from his shoulder and looked at him.

"Who's involved?" Mick asked. "You?"

"I wish it was me. God knows I do."

"Who?" Mick asked again.

"My baby," Charles said. "Carly."

Mick quickly lifted up and sat on the side of the bed. He continued to hold Rosalind's body in his arms as he lifted her with him. He remained inside of her. "Carly?" he asked, a look of concern blanketing his attractive face. He knew what that young lady meant to his brother. He knew all about the pedestal Charles put her on. "Carly killed a man?"

When Rosalind heard those words, she was floored too. "What?" she asked.

"Yes," Charles said into the phone, and Mick could hear the anguish in his voice. "I hate to say it with everything within me. But yes. Carly killed a man."

Mick thought for a moment. Rosalind was sitting straddle-style on top of him, with her face to his face. He had one hand cupping her bare ass. Another hand holding his cellphone. He repositioned her weight, as he contemplated the implications for his young niece. "Has she been arrested?" he finally asked his brother.

"No," Charles responded. "And she won't

be. I'll see to that. But we've got to get the body to Jericho, Mick."

Mick knew that was a cockamamie idea, but it wasn't the time nor the place. "Where are you?" he asked. "Where's the body?"

"It's here," Charles said. "At Carly's house in Boston."

"Who's there with you and Car?"

"Jenay and Brent."

"Don't involve anybody else," Mick said. "I'm on my way."

When the call ended, Mick attempted to pull out of Rosalind, but he couldn't. He began sliding her along his lap, moving her along his still-swollen shaft, until he came. He sputtered it out, and clenched, as he came. Then he leaned against her. "I've got to leave town," he said.

"I know. But you just got back."

He was exhausted. No doubt about that. But duty called. He slid out of her and stood up. He placed her back on their bed, kissed her on the lips, and then headed toward their bathroom.

Rosalind laid back down on the pillow his head had just left, smelling his cologne scent as she did, and watched his naked form retreat from her. "Where is they now?" she asked. "Jericho?"

"Boston," Mick responded, as he lifted the toilet seat and began peeing. "At Carly's house."

"Why did she do it?" she asked. "Did Big Daddy say?"

Mick leaned his head back and closed his eyes, as he shook off the last of his urine stream. "No," he said, his voice sounding anguished too. "But I will be finding out."

The drive from Philadelphia, where Mick lived, to Boston, where the incident occurred, generally took five-and-a-half hours. But Mick didn't drive, he flew on his private jet, and arrived in town in about an hour.

The vehicle waiting for him at the airstrip, a black SUV loaded with his Boston crew, drove casually to Carly's house. They had no clue why they were called in the middle of the night, and they loved their own lives too much to ask why. But they knew whatever the mission involved, it was big. Mick the Tick, their boss, didn't come himself on assignment unless it was too serious for them to handle alone, or too personal for them to execute.

And when the SUV drove onto the driveway of a lakefront home and stopped behind a Jaguar, Mick, seated in the front seat beside the driver, opened the door. "Wait here," he ordered his men, got out, and headed toward the house entrance. The door was opened from inside, and Mick, in black jeans, black boots and gloves, and a black bomber jacket, walked in.

His men looked at each other, wondering what the hell was going on, but they dared not speak about it. Their loyalty wasn't to each other, but to Mick, and to stay on his generous payroll they knew they had to keep it that way. They kept it that way.

Mick walked in as Charles opened the door. When the door was closed, Mick could see the strain on Charles's face. He actually had an urge to pull his big brother into his arms and comfort him. But neither he nor Charles ever learned how to show affection toward each other. Their background was too harsh and their dysfunctional parents were too cruel. They loved each other dearly, and was totally devoted to each other. But it always went without saying.

Charles began walking away. "He's in the kitchen," he said.

Mick followed his brother slowly, looking around at the clean, perfectly neat home. White walls. White furniture. White carpet. Too clean and neat, if you asked Mick. As if it wasn't somebody's home, but somebody's showcase. As if the person who lived here wasn't actually living here, but was putting on a show for people. That was the backstory. In situations like these, he always kept one in mind. But when they made their way into the kitchen, he saw the full story.

Beautiful Carly Sinatra was dressed now and sitting in a chair at her kitchen table, a glass of wine in front of her. Jenay had moved a chair next to her, and was seated beside her. Brent was seated at the table too, across from his stepmother and adopted sister, but rose to his feet when his uncle walked into the room. He was amazed that he could get to Boston so quickly. But he also knew that everybody didn't own a private jet like his uncle owned. Everybody wasn't able.

"Hello, sir," he said to Mick when he walked in. He wanted to give him a hug. He really loved his uncle, and had a kind of boyish enchantment with his larger-than-life persona. But he knew Mick was not that kind of man. Their relationship wasn't given to closeness or emotion, but to an almost super-formal respect.

Mick nodded in Brent's direction, but turned his attention, not to Carly, but to Jenay. He could see in her eyes the toll this was taking on her because he knew the signs. He saw it in his own wife often enough. "Hello, babe," he said to Jenay, leaned down, and actually hugged her.

Brent looked at his father, amazed by such a display of affection coming from a man like Mick. But Charles wasn't surprised. There was something about Jenay that endeared her to people. Mick was no exception.

Mick then took a look at the dead body. He walked over to the area, knelt down, and studied the wounds as if he was a medical examiner at a crime scene. Charles stood behind Jenay's chair and placed one hand on her shoulder and one hand on Carly's, as Mick did his inspection. It took longer than he thought it would. It was a clear-cut case as far as Charles was concerned. Besides, the manner of death wasn't the issue. Moving that body was. And the sooner, Charles felt, the better.

Mick finally stood up, stared down at the body a little longer still, and then walked over to the table. His eyes were riveted on Carly. "What happened?" he asked her.

"He tried," Brent started, but Charles held up a hand. He knew Mick. Mick wanted to hear it from the horse's mouth.

Carly sipped from her glass, as if to summon the courage to speak, and then spoke.

"He came over to thank me," she said.

"Thank you for what?" Mick asked, his eyes intense as he stared at her.

"For putting together a PR offensive that allowed him to get away with raping a thirteen-year-old girl."

Charles, Jenay, and Brent all looked at her. Say what now? That didn't sound like something *their* Carly would be a party to.

But Mick didn't seem surprised at all. "How did a thank you turn to this?"

"I told him to leave," Carly said. "I didn't want to have anything to do with him. But he wouldn't. When I went to phone the police, he knocked the phone out of my hand, and then tried to rape me."

"Unsuccessfully?" Mick asked.

Carly looked up at her uncle. "Yes. Of course." But that look she saw in his eyes was too all-knowing for her comfort level. As if he could see right through her. She quickly looked away from him.

Mick, however, continued to stare at her. "Did anybody know he was coming to visit you?"

"No," Carly said. "At least he implied no one did. He claimed he was driving around and decided to drop by."

"He was probably on the prowl for his next

victim," Jenay said, "and tried to make you his next one."

"Yes," Mick said, still staring at Carly. "More likely. Where is his car?"

"Across the street," Brent said.

"My men will get rid of it," Mick said, and then silence ensued.

Brent knew they had major work to do, and waited for his uncle to get the ball rolling. When he didn't do any such thing, he decided to do so himself. "We need to move the body," he said. "Once we get it to Jericho, we can have better control over the circumstances."

Mick looked at him. "How is that?"

"We talked about it," Brent said. "We've decided to put the body in one of the rooms at Dad's hotel. Dad and Carly will be there when Dad phone the police. Carly can claim the guy followed her to Jericho, like some stalker or somebody, she resisted his advances, and Dad walked in on him trying to rape her. We know there will be questions about the fact that his death was hours earlier, but Dad can claim he blacked out or something. He was that enraged. It won't hold water here in Boston. But we can make sure it will in Jericho. We can have control over the narrative in Jericho."

Mick looked at him. "Control?" he asked. "With a convoluted story like the one you just told me? With my brother's life on the line?" Mick shook his head. "No."

Charles was already studying his brother. "What do you suggest we do?" he asked.

"You and your family get on my plane and get your asses back to Jericho. Carly will remain in town, go to work as she normally does, and behave as shocked as everybody else when she hears the news that Campbell is missing. After the furor dies down, she will put in her two weeks' notice, citing family issues, and return to Jericho."

"But she doesn't want to stay here," Brent said. "It'll remind her of this night every time she stepped into this house."

"She won't see a single hair that will remind her of this night," Mick said. "My men will scrub it clean."

Brent frowned. "I'm not talking about any physical reminder. I'm talking about the emotional toll it will take on her."

Mick looked at Carly. "She will have to handle it," he said. "That's what happens when you stab somebody twenty-plus times. You have to handle the emotions."

Carly swallowed hard at the thought of reliving this night over and over and over again. She already had too many memories. Jenay pulled her closer. Brent looked at his father.

"Couldn't Carly come back to Jericho with us now, Dad?" he asked.

"She could," Charles said. "But suspicion would immediately fall to her if she were to abandon her job and leave town just as Ethan Campbell is reported missing. Mick is right. She has to stay, at least until the noise of his disappearance dies down."

"I'll stay here with her," Jenay said.

"No, you will not," Charles said firmly. "I'll not have you reliving this horror."

"But we can't leave her here alone."

"She won't be alone," Charles said. "I'll stay with her."

Both Brent and Jenay were shocked. Mick was too, but for a very different reason. He couldn't begin to understand a man who would leave his business for what could amount to an entire month to babysit his daughter.

Even Jenay understood the impracticality of it. "All I'm responsible for is the Inn, Charlie. You're responsible for all of it. All of your businesses and properties."

"That's what I'm thinking," Brent said. "It can't be done, Dad. How in the world are you going to stay away from Jericho for an entire month?"

"I'll deal with Jericho when I get back to Jericho. Right now my child needs me. I'm not letting Jenay deal with this, or you either, Brent. I'm staying with her. I'm taking care of her. I'll help her deal with it better than either one of you can. Because she can't just leave town. She has to stay here. I'm staying with her."

Brent exhaled. "How do you feel about that, Car? You're okay with staying here for what could end up being another month?"

Everybody looked at Carly. She thought about it. "There's no other way," she said. "Dad's right. They might believe me if I tell them what really happened. But they might not. If they don't, I'll go to prison for the rest of my life." She looked at her big brother, a man she also loved and respected. "What else can I do?"

Charles squeezed her shoulder. And looked at Mick. "You told us what we need to do. But what are we going to do about this body?"

Mick looked Charles dead in the eye. "I'll get rid of it," he said.

Carly looked at Jenay. But Jenay, and Brent, were staring at Charles. They took their cues from him.

Charles was in deep thought. "You feel disposal is better than Brent's plan?"

"Far better," Mick said. "Brent's plan

leaves out one glaring difference."

"What's that?" Charles asked.

"Carly didn't kill some average Joe. She killed Ethan Campbell." When Jenay looked at him surprised, Mick explained. "I know him because I know football. And I know his family is not going to sit back and let Maine dictate to them the circumstances of his death. They will hire their own forensic experts. They will hire their own team of lawyers. They will destroy you. You may think you're taking the fall for your daughter, but both of you may go down."

Brent and Jenay looked at Charles again. He let out an exhausted exhale and ran the back of his hand across his eyes. "That crossed my mind, too," he said.

"But what are you talking about doing?" Brent asked Mick. "You can't just get rid of a body."

Mick couldn't believe he said that. He gave Brent a chilling stare. "I can't?" he asked.

"But what I mean to say," Brent said, "is that his family will have questions when he turns up missing. And what about the inhumanity of what could be their lifelong uncertainty?"

But Charles looked at his son. "What do you think is the better alternative in a field of bad options? Me attempting to convince

Jericho, and Boston by the way, that I killed that man in defense of my daughter? Or that man disappearing from the face of this earth with his family wondering whatever happened to him?"

"And wondering it," Mick added, "with no tie-in to Carly or your father whatsoever. My way, Carly got rid of a scumbag and got to live another day. Your way, Carly got rid of a scumbag and your father, or Carly, or both might pay with their lives."

Brent ran his hand through his thick, black hair. He was already in too deep. "I'm a cop for crying out loud," his frustration forced him to say. "At least if we move the body there's some accountability. There's some closure for his family. It's still wrong, but . . . How can I be a party to what you're talking about?"

"Because you're my son," Charles answered instead of Mick, forcing Brent to look at him. "You have no choice."

Brent, still distressed, looked at Jenay.

"You have no choice," Jenay said too.

And Carly, hearing it all, burst into tears. "All of you are getting into all of this trouble," she said, "and it's all because of my actions. Because of me," she said harshly and hit herself, with a fist, in her chest. "Because of me!"

Charles quickly moved over, grabbed Carly from her chair, and lifted her into his arms. He held her and let her sob.

Brent began to pace, with his hand still raking through his hair, and Jenay placed her elbow on the table, with her chin in her hand, and closed her eyes.

Charles, instinctively feeling her distress, took one of his hands and prodded her to her feet. When she rose, he pulled her into his arms too.

Brent stood against the wall, his head back, staring at his uncle. He was amazed at how calm Mick was. He was all-business, with no emotion whatsoever, at a time like this. As if disposing of bodies were nothing new to him.

But it was new to them, and they could hardly bear it. Brent walked over to his family, to his father, his mother, and his sister, and wrapped his arms around them all.

MALLORY MONROE

CHAPTER EIGHT

Two Months Later

She didn't think it would make it, but it did. All the way from Baltimore, Maryland. But as she drove into the parking lot of the Saint Catherine's Episcopal Church in Jericho County, her vintage Mustang was the least of her concerns. She had been ordered by Bishop Lanier to vacate her post as Dean of Students at Saint Catherine's Prep Academy in Baltimore, the largest school in the diocese, to come to a small, failing school in Maine. She knew why. She knew what happened with Kent caused her relocation. But knowing why didn't make it feel any better. And as she sat in her Mustang and watched the tall, white, steeple church in front of her, she felt that sense of failure all over again. She was on the fast track to glory just a few weeks ago. Now she was on a backroad to nowhere. How did everything go so wrong?

And how were this new staff going to feel about her sudden appointment? From everything she could gather, every school master they had ever had in their eighty-year history had always been male, white, and old. Every single one. How were they going to feel about a young, black woman taking over?

Not that it mattered how they felt, she decided, as she grabbed her attaché case off of the passenger seat and got out of the car. The Bishop appointed her. Saint Catherine's wasn't self-sufficient: it belonged to the diocese. They had no choice.

But when she entered the vestibule of the century-old church, and made her way into the sanctuary where members of the vestry were there to greet her, the sense of purpose she felt began to waver. The vestry was ten-person strong and, from what she could see when she entered, every one of them were either old, very old, or decrepit, and all of them were white. She knew they wouldn't be a super-diverse group, this was *Maine* after all, but she didn't expect total uniformity. Why in the world, she wondered, as she made her way down the aisle, did the Bishop in all of his infinite wisdom appoint somebody like her to come to a place like this? It seemed like a monumental mix match!

The members of the vestry sat in chairs at the very front of the church and every one of them appeared to be as surprised by the view as she was. Some even looked at each other, as if to confirm that others saw what they were seeing. They knew a woman was coming. Her name made that clear. But apparently, she realized as she walked, they had no idea the woman would be this young and, undoubtedly, this *black*. But she had a job to do. She kept on walking.

A gray-haired man was the only one to smile. He stood up, clasped his hands together, and then hurried to greet her. "You must be our new Headmaster," he said. Then he smiled nervously, stopped in his tracks, as his face began turning beet-red. "Head*mistress*," he corrected himself. And then he continued to hurry toward her, extending his hand. "I'm Joe Huddleson. The parish priest. The priest in charge, actually, of both church and school up until your appointment. Welcome to Saint Catherine's!"

"Thank you," she said as she removed her attaché case from her right hand to her left, and shook his hand. "I'm Sharon Flannigan."

He was all smiles as they shook, and welcoming in tone, but she could see the reluctance even in him. He was the man in charge of a failing school. She was replacing him. She understood his reluctance. But unlike Joe, the rest of the members, most of whom were women, weren't even pretending. They seemed to be too busy experiencing the shock of it all.

Joe continued. "Once I introduce you to our church leadership, and after a morning assembly where you will get to meet all of the school staff, and after I give you the grand tour of the church and school." He paused, catching his breath. Then added: "Such as it is. We are, I am quite sure, a far cry from what you are used to in a big city like Baltimore. But after all of that, after all of the introductions and tours and the meet and greet of staff, I will be happy to escort you to the Inn."

Sharon was confused. "The Inn?"

"The Jericho Inn, why yes. A bed and breakfast here. Given your . . . *um*. Your . . . *um*. How shall I say it? Given your gender, yes, your *gender*, we felt it would be unwise, or it would be best for you to select where you would prefer to live. We did not want to be presumptuous and select a place for you. And the Rectory will not do. And now, looking at you," he said with a smile, "I think it was quite a stroke of genius actually."

"A stroke of genius?" Sharon asked. She never cared for hyperbole. "In what way?"

Joe cleared his throat. He was most uncomfortable and Sharon couldn't figure out why. Was it because of her sex, her race, her age? All of the above? None of the above? Then she decided it didn't matter either way.

"What I meant to say is that I think you will feel right at home at the Inn." Joe pulled out a handkerchief and began wiping his forehead. The man was so nervous he was literally sweating. With him in charge, Sharon thought, there was no wonder the school was failing. Was the rest of the leadership this rubber-backed?

He continued. "What I meant to say is that the lady who runs the Inn, Jenay Sinatra, is a most welcoming sort of person. And the Inn itself is a lovely place. You will be comfortable there. That is what I meant to say."

Sharon could tell he meant to say a whole lot more, but she wasn't there to quiver with him or anyone else. She had a job to do and she was going to give it her all. It felt like starting at the bottom again, but she was used to that too. A desire to know this man's deeper thoughts, or even the thinking among the vestry members as a whole, was a total waste of time. "Perhaps you can introduce me to the leadership here assembled," she said, "and we can move on from there?"

He smiled, relieved. "Yes. Let's. Get on with it, that is!" Then he cleared his throat.

"Right this way, please," he said, motioning his hand for her to follow.

And Sharon followed his lead. She followed him down the aisle and smiled as she went. She was here now. The Bishop had demoted her and relocated her. She had no choice either.

"Eat it all, Nita," Jenay said to her youngest child as she poured herself another cup of coffee. "I didn't give you that much."

"When are you going to sign it, Mommy?" Bonita Sinatra asked as she ate.

"Let Carly sign it."

"She cannot anymore," Bonita said. "She signed the last one, but she cannot sign this one."

Jenay looked at her daughter. "And why is that?"

"Because my teacher said one of my parents have to sign it, and Carly is not my parent."

"She lives in your same household, she's an adult, and she's your sister. What's the difference?"

"My teacher said she is not my parent. She cannot sign anymore."

"Give that junk to me," Ashley said with a whimsical smile on her face, as Donald laughed. "I'm good at faking Ma's signature. I'll sign it for you."

"You will do no such thing, Ashley," Jenay said. And then reached her hand toward Bonita. "Hand it here."

Bonita smiled as she gladly handed the three-page field trip authorization to her mother. Jenay smiled when Bonita smiled. Mainly because Bonita had blossomed into a beautiful little girl with long, light-brown hair down her back, and the most pleasant of personalities.

They were in the kitchen. Jenay was standing at the center island, while Bonita, Carly, Ashley, and Donald, the Sinatra children who still lived at home, were sitting around it. Everybody were eating the breakfast Jenay had prepared. Except Jenay, who never cared for breakfast.

"They make you sign your life away," Donald said. "Don't they, Ma?"

"It's all about their liability," Jenay responded as she sipped coffee and continued to read the paperwork. "It's all about them."

Carly, reading yet another book on her IPad, looked up at the clock over the stove. "Is that time right?" she asked.

"It's right," Donald said as he looked at his adopted sister. He was always amazed by her

93

beauty. She was even more beautiful than Ashley. He would have been proud to introduce her to some of his male friends. But she was always so serious and stern, as if she was better than the rest of them, that he never bothered. "That time is right. Dad's just late as usual."

But Carly knew she had better finish eating before their father came downstairs, so that she didn't add to his tardiness. She put down her IPad, and began eating her food more vigorously.

Ashley stared at Carly too. She was always an oddball to Ash, even when they were kids, so her current odd behavior was par for the course to her. But it still was curious. "Why don't you buy yourself a new car?" she asked her. "You're working now. Dad got you that teaching job at Saint Catherine's, a job you said you wanted. Instead of putting that hunk of junk of yours in the shop for repairs, you should have bought yourself a real car. I'll help you look."

"Thanks," Carly said, "but no thanks."

"Why the hell not, Carly?" Ashley asked. "You can afford it. You gave up that cushy job in Boston to come back here to Jericho, which still doesn't make sense to me. But why wouldn't you splurge a little?"

Carly didn't respond to that. Nobody knew about her mishap in Boston outside of her parents, her big brother Brent, and her uncle, the mobster Mick Sinatra. And she aimed to keep it that way.

But Ashley and Donald smelled a rat, and wouldn't stop questioning her about it every chance they could. "Why did you come back here anyway?" Donald asked, picking up the torch.

"I told you why. I wanted to be close to home."

"That makes no sense at all," Ashley said. "Boston is only a couple hours away. You could come home every day if you wanted to. You didn't have to quit your job."

Jenay glanced over at Carly, and saw her distress. "Leave her alone," she said to Ash and Donald. "Sometimes people need a change of pace. That's why she didn't want to work for Daddy. She's tired of the corporate world."

"But why is she so tired?" Donald asked. "That's the big question. And what does being tired of the corporate world have to do with buying a car? When she first came back to Jericho, I understood it. Maybe she needed more stability before she bought a car. But she has a job now."

"Not to mention that big, fat bank account she brought back with her from Boston," Ashley added.

"It wasn't all that fat," Carly interjected.

"But it's fat enough to buy a car," Ashley said. "If I can buy a car on the salary Dad pays me, I know you can buy one from all that big money you were making in Boston."

"Leave her alone," Jenay said again without looking up from her reading this time. "She has a car. It's just in the shop."

"She doesn't have a car, Ma," Donald said. "She has a hunk of junk. That car is as old as I am. She needs a car and we all know it."

"And she'll buy one when she's good and ready," Jenay said and then looked at Donald. "Leave her alone."

Donald knew when to cool it with his stepmother and boss. But he also knew how to change the subject without changing the subject. "It doesn't matter anyway," he said, "since Dad let's her drive his luxurious Jaguar all over town like she's his equal. He never let me drive it once. Even when my car got---" Donald hesitated.

Ashley looked at her brother and smiled. "Go on and say it, boy."

"Even when my car got repossessed. Okay? I said it! But I'll get another one when

I'm back on my feet again, so it's no big deal. But even then, when Dad knew I was struggling, he didn't come to my rescue."

"Perhaps because you had no business struggling," Carly said. "You made more than enough money as General Manager at the Inn to pay your bills. You chose not to."

Ashley smiled. "She's right about that, Donnie."

"But regardless of all of that," Donald said to Carly, as he was never willing to face his own demons, "Dad didn't offer to help me."

"He even offered to buy her a car when she first came back home," Ashley said. "Did you know that?"

"Hell yeah I knew it," Donald said. "And for reasons I'll never understand until the day I die, Miss Carly turned him down."

"Yeah, right?" Ashley said with a smile. "That amazes me still! Let Dad offer to buy me a new car. Man, I'd be at that car lot hours before it opens. I'll spend the night there waiting to get my new ride!"

"But it's true," Donald said to Carly. "You, Tony and Brent get preferential treatment, I'm telling you. Dad treats the three of you differently than the rest of us."

"For real though," Ashley said. "Mom at least lets us drive her Mercedes. She treats all of us the same. But Dad doesn't allow me nor Donnie anywhere near his car."

"Bobby either," Donald added, still looking at Carly. "Yet you can just pop up from out of nowhere when me, Ash, and Bobby have been living in Jericho all along. We've been working for Dad and Mom, doing what they need us to do. But you show up and he all but turns the keys to the kingdom over to you. He treats us, especially me, differently than he treats you."

"Maybe it has less to do with the fact that he treats you differently, Don," Carly said, "and more to do with the fact that you have no job and haven't shown yourself responsible enough."

"I do have a job, for your information," Donald corrected her. Then he added, in a more subdued tone: "Just not the same job."

Ashley laughed. "Don't try to sugarcoat it, bud. Your little antics with Biker Chick got your butt demoted. You went from General Manager of the Jericho Inn to desk clerk supervisor. That's a hellava fall, my brother, even in my eyes."

"He better be glad Ma didn't fire him altogether," Carly said. "If he worked on my staff and pulled a stunt like the one he pulled, where he didn't show up for work for three days straight without even calling or letting someone know where he could be reached, I wouldn't have demoted him. I would have terminated him immediately."

"That'll never happen," Donald said, "because I'll never work for your stuck-up butt in a million years."

"Since I'll never hire yours in a zillion years," Carly retorted, "then I guess neither one of us have anything to worry about."

"Stop arguing," Bonita said. "You and Donnie argue too much."

Ashley laughed. Donald rolled his eyes. Carly picked back up her IPad to continue to read her book, and occasionally eat.

Then they all heard the loud voice of their father yelling down from upstairs. *"Jenay?"* he blared. *"Jenay?"*

Jenay didn't bother to look up. *"What?"* she blared back as she began signing Bonita's paperwork.

"Come here! *Jenay?"*

Jenay handed the paperwork back to Bonita. "Don't lose that," she said, took another sip of her coffee, and then made her way upstairs.

"I don't get it," Ashley said. "All Dad has to do is tell her to come, and she drops everything and take off."

Donald looked at Ash. "So?"

Ashley looked at him sidelong. "So? If that was my husband, I'd ask him what was wrong with his two legs. And then I'd tell him to bring his ass to me." Donald laughed.

Carly shook her head. "That's why not one of those men you date day in and day out has asked you to marry him." Donald laughed even harder.

"No, you didn't say that to me!" Ashley responded, smiling too. "At least I have prospects, Miss Bookworm. All you have are books!"

"Read one," Carly said. "You might actually enjoy it."

"Kiss this," Ashley retorted, lifting her butt toward her sister. "You might actually enjoy it."

Donald laughed again. He loved both of his adopted sisters fiercely, although he made it his mission to never let that uppity Carly ever know his true feelings. "You're always good for a laugh, Ash," he said heartily.

CHAPTER NINE

"Charlie, aren't you going to be late?" Jenay asked as she walked across the landing into the master bedroom. But she stopped talking and walking when she looked up. When she saw Charles naked and lying across the bed, his feet on the floor, rubbing his dick, her vagina tingled.

"Lock the door," he said.

If he was up to anything else, Jenay would have protested vigorously. They both had jobs to get to. But Charles had a way of bringing out the lust in her unlike any other man ever could. On sight he could give her a rise. And just seeing him, just seeing his penis, made her so filled with lust that she could hardly get to him fast enough.

She locked the door and walked up to him. He opened his legs. She stood between them and untied her robe, revealing her own naked body.

"That's right, baby," Charles said. "You know what I want."

Jenay knelt down, placed his cock in her mouth, and began to lick it.

Charles leaned back and felt the sensual texture of her tongue as it slowly slid over the ridges of his penis. And when she put it into her mouth, he could feel the muscles of his thighs tighten. He never dreamed he would want to be with a woman as badly as he wanted Jenay. In his player days, he was not a kind lover. He was good in bed, but not kind. And he always knew there was a difference. Because with Jenay, he was living the difference. The way she made him feel could not be verbalized. Just felt to the roots of his hair. And he felt her now. He felt her tongue, her touch, her mastery of his body and mind.

And when she looked up at him, as if she could instinctively feel the emotions he was feeling for her, and he saw her big, brown expressive eyes, he took her by the arms and pulled her up the length of his body, until she was sitting on his lap. Her legs were on either side of his thighs, as he pulled her further down, and began sucking her breasts. Then he moved up to her mouth, and kissed her for a long time. Until he knew he couldn't hold out much longer.

He lifted her ass so that when she came back down, she was sliding down on his rod. He let out a heavy sigh when she slid down and down and down until his cock was all the way deep inside of her.

Jenay felt it too as she slid down his long rod. And when she began to move up and down, along the length, she closed her eyes and enjoyed him. Her breasts were bouncing so much as she rode him, that he took his hands and squeezed them. But they continued to bounce in his hands. They were that big. And he loved it. He loved it so much that he pulled her down again, and sucked her as she fucked him.

When they came, it was as magical as it could ever be. They came hard and they came together. Charles pulled her in his arms and took over. His strokes increased as he poured into her, and she wanted to cry out with joy. But she knew the children were downstairs. She held her peace. And he continued to fuck her hard.

Downstairs, Ashley had finished eating and was grabbing her purse. "I'm out," she said as she began to leave. "Bye, Nita."

"Bye, Ashley," Bonita responded. "Be good."

"Why are you leaving all of a sudden?" Donald asked, still stuffing his face with food. "Aren't you going to drop me off, Ash?"

"Then come on! Dad said if I'm late one

more time I'm fired. He can be late all the time, but if I'm late he threatens to fire me."

Carly could hardly believe it. "He owns the company, Ash, why are you comparing yourself to him? He owns the company."

"So?" Ashley asked. "What does that have to do with anything? Late is late. What's the difference?"

If she didn't know that difference, Carly thought, then she would be wasting her time explaining it. So she didn't bother.

"Come on, Donnie, I mean it!" Ashley said, as she hurried out of the door.

Carly watched as Donald drank the last of his juice and hurriedly ate another spoonful of egg. "If I were you," he said as he ate, "I'd take Dad up on his offer and get that new car. You're crazy not to." Then he kissed Bonita goodbye, and took off.

Carly shook her head. If that boy only knew how little she cared about some car, or any other material thing right now, he'd stop bringing it up. But she didn't try to enlighten him. She let him go.

Bonita looked at Carly. "They are always late," she said.

"Yes, they are," Carly agreed, with a smile.

"That's why I like you the most," Bonita said. "You're never late. You never make mistakes."

Carly had a sudden flash of that knife coursing through Ethan Campbell's back, and the way his knees bent when she pulled it out. And Nita thought she was the perfect one? "Finish your food," she said to her kid sister.

Charles and Jenay, showered and fully dressed in their respective business suits, arrived downstairs some ten minutes after Ashley and Donald left. When Charles saw Carly sitting at the center island, staring at seemingly nothingness, he touched Jenay on the arm and pulled her back. When Jenay looked at him, he nodded toward Carly.

Jenay saw the staring and nodded too. "She's been doing that a lot lately."

Charles looked at Jenay. "Does she talk to you about it?"

"That's the sad part," Jenay said. "She won't tell me a thing. She won't tell anybody. She keeps it all locked in. Sometimes I wonder if she's still reliving that hellish night, and reliving it over and over and over again."

Charles opened his suitcoat, placed his hands on his hips, and exhaled, as they both continued to watch their daughter. "I'm worried about her, Jenay," he said. "I'd be lying if I said otherwise. She seem so normal when I'm talking with her and when she's one-on-one with others. But when she's alone, and she doesn't know that she's being watched, she seem to be in such pain."

"Poor baby," Jenay said. "There's a lot going on inside of her, but she won't say what. I still think she should go to therapy."

Charles looked at Jenay. "And say what? She can't tell them anything about what happened that night. She can't even hint about it. And please don't hand me that nonsense about how they can't tell. They can tell the authorities if a crime has been committed, or something like that. Therapy is out."

"I hear what you're saying," Jenay said. "But she doesn't have to talk about that night. I think Carly had a lot going on internally long before that night in Boston."

Charles nodded. "That's true."

"But it doesn't matter. She tells me no repeatedly when I ask her to at least consider seeing a therapist. Or even Tony. He's a clinical psychologist. I asked her to at least go and talk to him."

"She refused?"

"Yup. She declares she's fine. She's real good at declaring that."

Charles nodded. "Yes, she is," he admitted.

"Anyway," Jenay said. "I'd better go." She leaned over and kissed Charles on the lips. Charles pulled her back, and kissed her again.

Jenay then walked toward the front door. "Bonita?" she yelled. "Come on!"

Carly broke her stare when she heard Jenay's voice, and Bonita jumped down from her chair, grabbed her book bag, and hurried toward her parents.

"My baby!" Charles said as he lifted her into his arms.

"Bye, Daddy!" Bonita said. "You be good today."

Charles laughed. "If you will, I will," he said as he put her down.

"I will," Bonita said.

"Then I will," Charles responded.

"We're leaving, Car," Jenay yelled toward the kitchen, and Carly turned toward her. "See you tonight."

"Have a good day," Carly said, rising, and Jenay and Bonita hurried out.

Carly began grabbing her purse and IPad. "Ready, Dad?" she asked as she headed his way.

"I'm ready," Charles said as he watched Carly head his way. She was smiling now, as if her somber mood never happened. When she arrived, they hugged.

"Thanks for letting me use your car today," she said when they stopped embracing. "Milt said mine should be ready in a few more days."

"No problem," Charles responded. He kept an arm around her waist. "If I hadn't left my truck at the office, you could have already been on your way."

"How did that have happened anyway? How could you leave your truck?"

"Your mother picked me up at the office because we had a meeting to attend. After the meeting we got lazy and decided to just come on home. But you don't mind dropping me off first, do you?"

"Not at all! We're late, but it's no big deal," she added.

Charles was surprised. "Late? But I thought you didn't have to be to work until 9?"

"I'm not talking about me," Carly said with a smile. "I'm talking about you. I said *we* so you wouldn't feel bad."

Charles laughed and pulled her closer. "You're a good kid, Carly," he said. "I'm proud to have you as my daughter." Then a serious look came onto Charles's face. "Don't you ever forget that."

Carly looked at Charles. Here was a man, she thought, who took an entire month out of his life to spend it cooped up in her house in

Boston, all for her sake. Here was a man who was not even a blood relative, but yet treated her better than her biological parents ever did. And her heart swelled with emotion. He was the very reason she hadn't completely given up on men. "Thanks, Dad," she said heartfelt.

But Charles continued to look at her with concern in his eyes. "You're okay?" he asked.

At first it seemed as if she would crack, and tell him how she really felt. But then she reverted back to form. "Oh, yes," she said bluntly, as if it was an obvious fact. "I'm great." Then she smiled again, and headed out of the front door.

She was a long way from great, and Charles knew it, as he followed her out.

CHAPTER TEN

The Jaguar lumbered along the streets of
Jericho and Charles, with sunglasses covering
his eyes, took peeps at Carly. She sat quietly
on the passenger seat, reading from her IPAD.
She looked like a typical school teacher in her
tucked-in brown blouse, cardigan sweater, and
pencil skirt. Her long hair was pulled back into
a thick ponytail. But her outer appearance was
the only thing typical about her that Charles
could see. Because looking deeper told a
different story. She never fielded messages on
her cell phone the way women her age always
did. She turned down every guy that asked her
out, and refused to hang out with any of the
single ladies around town. Even when her car
wouldn't crank and had to be towed to the
shop, she refused his offer to buy her a new
car. She refused to let him buy her a house.
She lived at home and preferred it that way.
He used to think it was because she needed the
closeness of her family to help her overcome
what that tragedy in Boston might have done
to her. But now he wasn't so sure.

He turned a corner, and looked at her

again. "What are you reading?"

"Loving the Head Man."

Charles suddenly thought about what Jenay had done to him that morning. "Head? As in?"

Carly smiled. "The boss, Dad. It's about loving the boss."

Charles smiled. "Ah. A romance novel?"

"Right."

"Most girls your age wouldn't be reading about romance. They'd be out there living it."

Carly looked up, her big, sincere eyes on full display. "I'm hardly like most girls my age, Dad," she said honestly.

Charles's heart squeezed when she made that declaration. He waited for more. He waited for her to say that most girls her age didn't have a murder under their belt, but she didn't go there. She never went there with him. "So how are things going with you overall?" he asked. "Teaching in a small, private school in Jericho is a far cry from running a PR department in Boston."

"That is true," Carly said, still reading.

Charles waited for more, but nothing came. Yep, he thought sadly, as he turned another corner. Great his ass. She was a long way from great.

He looked at her again. "I still want you to

consider coming to work for me, darling." She looked up. "When you're ready."

"I know," she said. "And I probably will. When I think I'm ready for the grind again. Teaching presents the right level of stress for me right now. Not too much, and not too little. The kids are sweet. I can deal with my co-workers pretty well. This is what I need right now."

Charles nodded. Carly always had that clarity of thought whenever she chose to share it with him. "Understood," he said.

She smiled. "But it is rather odd, don't you think?"

Charles looked at her. "What is?"

"You already have Ash, Donald, and Bobby working for you. Three of your children. Aren't they enough?"

"No," Charles said bluntly. "The three I want, you, Anthony, and Brent, are charting your own path. Instead I'm stuck with Robert, who pays more attention to his ladies than his job. Ashley, who pays more attention to her men than her job. And Donald, who pays more attention to anything other than his job."

Carly smiled.

"They're good kids," Charles continued. "I love them to death. But they're badly distracted and I don't see an end to that distraction anytime soon. It's you that I want. You, Brent, and Tony. You guys are dependable. You're leaders. You're the ones who can carry on the family business, and your less-focused siblings, right along with it."

"Thanks, Dad, for the vote of confidence. I really appreciate it."

"But?" Charles asked.

"I'm not ready yet," she said sincerely.

Charles nodded. "Good enough. But when you are ready to return to the corporate world, you give me first dibs, you hear?"

Carly laughed. "I hear," she said.

But when Charles turned the corner onto the street where his downtown office was located, and saw a small group of protesters in front of his office, his face went from a smile to a frown. "What the hell?" he asked rhetorically. Then he lifted his sunglasses off of his face and placed them on top of his head, for a better look.

"What?" Carly asked, looking too. When she saw the assembled group, she was surprised. "Protestors?"

"Yes," Charles said with anger in his voice as he sped up to the curb in front of his storefront office, stopped his Jaguar with an abrupt stop, and jumped out.

Carly's heart began to pound. She knew

there was a lot of tension in town because of the election season that was still in full bloom, as candidate after candidate attempted to portray the Sinatra name as if it were synonymous with greed and excess and everything else that was wrong in their town. Her father, especially, had to endure withering attacks, and he was enduring it with class, she thought. But even she would agree that this protest in front of his place of business was taking it too far.

"What do you think you're doing?" Charles asked as he began walking toward the protestors. "This is private property."

"My name is Abe Norris," the leader walked up to him and said. "I am here to tell you, Mr. Sinatra, that your days of tyranny are about to come to an end."

"This is private property," Charles said. "I want you off of it now."

Norris lifted up his bullhorn. "This building may belong to you," he said into the horn, "but you don't own this sidewalk. You may think you own this city, but you don't own us!"

The protestors cheered.

"Get the hell away from my office," Charles warned, "and I mean now."

"You may own this building," Norris said again into his bullhorn, "but you don't own this sidewalk. You may own this city," he continued, but Charles angrily grabbed his bullhorn, broke it across his knee, and then tossed the remains into the street. The protestors, seeing his anger and suddenly realizing who they were dealing with, backed up. Even their leader backed up.

"Now get the hell away from my office before I break more than that horn!" Charles blared. When he moved as if he was going to attack them, they ran.

But Norris held his ground, and glared at Charles. "Make me," he said with clenched teeth.

Charles went up to him. He grabbed Norris by the catch of his shirt and began dragging him off of the sidewalk. Norris tried to hit back, but Charles was pure muscle and Norris was hurting his own fists more than he was hurting Charles. When Charles threw him into the street, causing him to scrape his hands, he could hardly believe the treatment.

"You won't get away with this, Big Daddy!" Norris yelled derisively as he stood back up. "I'll cut you down to size one of these days, boy. I'm going to cut you down to size!"

"Fine," Charles said. "Just keep your ass away from my property while you're doing all of your cutting!"

Norris snatched up his broken bullhorn and then made his way across the street too. But when he saw the beautiful black lady get out of Charles's Jaguar, his walked slowed. When he arrived on the opposite side of the street, he pulled one of the male protestors aside.

"Yes, he's always like that," the protestor said, anticipating the question. "That's why nobody can stand his ass. He broke your bullhorn without even caring that it wasn't his property he was breaking. But he's always been that way. Arrogant prick!"

But Norris was still looking at Carly. "Who is that?" he asked, motioning toward her.

The protestor, however, was surprised. "You aren't from around here," he said. "Are you?"

Norris paused, then decided to speak. "In every protest, the person being protested love to blame outside agitators for all of the confusion. Well, I'm a true outside agitator. I travel this land agitating for citizens' rights."

"But not for nothing. Am I right?" the protestor asked. "Cruikshank's campaign hired you, didn't they?"

Norris paused again. Then spoke. "I don't discuss my employer," he said.

"But why did they hire you? I know they want you to agitate Big Daddy Sinatra. But agitate him into doing what?"

"Just agitate him. Because guess what? That bullhorn breaking he just did? The way he threw me in the street like I was lower than a dog? It was secretly videotaped and will undoubtedly lead every newsbreak all day, and every newspaper headline tomorrow morning around these parts. You think he's hated now, you just wait. The strong arm of Big Daddy Sinatra will be exposed, and it will be exposed in vivid color." Then Norris looked at the protestor. "I know what I'm doing, pal."

The protestor laughed.

"Now answer a question for me," Norris said. "Who's that lady?"

The protestor looked as Carly began getting into the driver side of the Jaguar, and Big Daddy stood beside the car talking with her. "That's his daughter," he said.

Norris smiled. "Go on!"

"No, I'm serious. He adopted her. And adores her. He has a lot of kids, probably more than meets the eye given his reputation, but that one over there is his heart."

"Well," Norris said with a contemplative look, as if an entirely new avenue of agitation had just opened up for him. "You don't say?" he added.

The grade-school students marched in a straight line toward the auditorium. Carly was just entering the hall, just arriving to work, when she saw them, and then the teachers following behind them. "What's going on?" she asked Judea, the nearest teacher, as she fell in line too.

"Our new boss is about to be introduced," Judea said.

"Is it a woman like they claimed it was going to be?"

"I haven't met her yet. But I think so."

Just as they were about to continue, Penelope Wright, one of the vestry members, walked over to the two of them. "Miss Sinatra," she said. "May I have a word?"

Carly glanced at Judea. Penelope Wright barely spoke to her on any given day. Now she wanted to speak privately with her? "Of course," Carly said and followed the old lady away from the others.

"How are you today?" Penelope asked.

"Very well, thank you," Carly said. "How may I help you?"

"I see your father has put his foot in it again. They had a live report on the morning news. He didn't have to break that man's megaphone, or push him down. What is wrong with that man?"

"Is my father the reason you wish to speak privately with me?" Carly asked her. "Because if it is," she continued, but Penelope interrupted her.

"No, no, it isn't about him," Penelope said. "It just angers me sometimes the level of behavior he stoops to. As a leader in our community, he should know better. But this isn't about him. It's about you. It's about you doing the vestry a favor."

That request was even more shocking to Carly than her indictment of her father. "A favor?" she asked.

"Let me explain. The new head mistress, Miss Flannigan, will be staying at your father's hotel. At the Jericho Inn. We thought, given your familial relationship with the owner, that you would be the best person to escort her over there and introduce her to Mrs. Sinatra. If you don't mind."

Carly smiled. "Not at all," she said. It was a reasonable request. "I'll be honored to do so."

Penelope smiled. "Good," she said. "You have always been an outstanding person, Carly. That is why we didn't hesitate to hire you. Big Daddy may have asked us to consider you, but he does not run Saint Catherine's the way he runs the rest of this town. We hired you in spite of him. Thank you," she said, and left.

Carly shook her head. What did her father ever do to that woman? Sometimes she could be so reasonable, like her request for Carly to escort the new head mistress, and other times she could be the most unbearably obnoxious woman she'd ever met.

But when Carly fell back in line, and made her way into the auditorium, she realized that she was wrong. As soon as she saw the new head mistress, and especially saw the skin color of the new head mistress, she fully understood why Penelope Wright singled her out to be the woman's escort. She clearly saw that Penelope Wright wasn't being reasonable at all. Just, as she usually was, obnoxious.

CHAPTER ELEVEN

"This is our chain of command," Marla Grape said to the new clerk, showing her the hierarchical tree on the front desk computer. "If a complaint comes in, you contact me. Always come to me first because I'm the lead clerk. But if I'm not available, you move up the chain, as you can see here, to Mr. Sinatra."

Becky Hamlisch, the new clerk, looked at the older woman. "*Mister* Sinatra?" she asked. "You mean Donnie?"

Marla shook her head. "No, I do not mean *Donnie*. I mean Mr. Sinatra. I know everybody thinks of him as one of them, but he is still the desk clerk supervisor of this hotel. He's *Mister* Sinatra to you and me and everybody else who works here."

"I didn't mean any disrespect," Becky quickly stated, distressed by Marla's response. "Honest I didn't. He told me to call him Donnie, that's the only reason I said it like that."

"I know what he told you," Marla said, "but I'm telling you that calling our boss by his first name is not acceptable. And don't you worry.

If he has a problem with that, tell him to come see me."

Becky smiled. "Yes, ma'am," she said.

As they continued to stand behind the counter inside the lobby of the Jericho Inn, a bed and breakfast in the heart of town, and continued to discuss more of Becky's job duties, a big Ford F-150 drove up and could be seen through the double doors of the front entrance. When Becky looked up and saw the truck, she stiffened. "A customer just pulled up, Miss Marla," she said anxiously. "My first customer. What do I do? What am I supposed to do first?"

"Settle down," Marla admonished her, as she continued to input keys. "That's what you do first. It's no big deal. You're going to have customers every single workday I assure you."

Becky smiled, realizing her overreaction. "Yes, ma'am," she said.

Then Marla looked up too. When she saw Charles Sinatra get out of the truck, she looked back down and continued to key-in. "That's not a customer, anyway," she said. "That's Big Daddy."

Becky looked at the handsome, muscular man as he stood beside his truck and put on his suit coat. "Big Daddy?" she asked. He wore shades, an obviously expensive suit, and was dripping sex appeal even from a distance away. Becky was in her thirties now, and still had high hopes of marrying well. "Who's Big Daddy?"

"Oh, no one special," Marla said sarcastically. "He's just the owner of this place."

Becky looked at her. "The owner? But I thought Donnie's stepmom, I mean Mr. Sinatra's stepmom, owned this hotel."

"She runs this hotel. But Big Daddy owns it. He owned it before he married her."

Becky was surprised. "That's Mrs. Sinatra's husband?"

Marla nodded. "Yes. And it still drives these ladies around here crazy. An outsider like her corralling a man like him. But there's no doubt about it. He's all hers, and she's all his. Every woman that's tried to break that bond have the scars to prove it."

Becky was disappointed. Jenay Sinatra, she'd already decided, was nobody's pushover. But Becky was no bad looker either. Most men considered her most attractive. She still held out hope. And when he entered the B & B, she couldn't help but smile. "He's very good looking," she said to Marla.

"He's mean as a hungry lion on a summer night," Marla replied. "That's why they call him Big Daddy. It's not an affectionate term, I assure you. He never shows an ounce of compassion ever. He kicks people out of his rent houses like they were roaches to him. You should have seen what he did to a protestor this morning. It was all over the news. He nearly killed that man."

Becky looked at her. "Really?"

"He's worse than the government. He's worse than Big Brother. He just takes and takes and is trying to take over this whole town."

"And that's why they call him Big Daddy?"

"Exactly why. No ma'am, there is nothing affectionate about that term, or that man, I assure you." Then Marla looked at Becky. "But don't you dare call him Big Daddy to his face. He doesn't like it. He's Mister Sinatra to you."

"But I thought Donnie was Mister Sinatra to me," Becky reminded her.

"They both are," Marla said, and then smiled a big smile as Charles finally made his way to the front desk. "Good afternoon, sir!" she said with exaggerated joy.

"Good afternoon," Charles Sinatra said as he approached. Becky noticed immediately that he wasn't returning Marla's gaiety. This man was all business. Mean, Becky thought, just like Marla said. "Is she in?" he asked.

"Yes, sir," Marla said. "She's in her office,

sir. She and Mr. Sinatra are reviewing the protocol list for the upcoming debutante ball."

But Charles frowned. "She and *who* are reviewing the list?" he asked.

Marla swallowed hard. "She and Donnie, sir," she said.

"Oh," Charles said, and Becky stifled a grin. Charles looked at her, and removed his shades.

When she saw his beautiful green eyes, her heartbeat quickened. And just by his look alone, she was pleased to see that he was sizing her up as most men did. He even looked downward, which was always, to her, a sign of more than a passing interest. And she could tell, by his reaction when he looked, that he liked what he saw.

"Oh, I'm sorry," Marla said, when she realized Charles had no clue who this new face was working in his hotel. "I want you to meet Becky Hamlisch, sir." Marla motioned toward Becky. "She's our new desk clerk."

Becky was about to extend her hand, but when she didn't see Charles extending his, she quickly thought the better of it. "Nice to meet you, sir."

"Nice to meet you," Charles said sincerely, but without puff or smiling, which she respected.

"You have a beautiful hotel here. It is very

well run."

"Credit my wife for that," Charles said. "It was a big pile of crap when I first got my hands on it, and very poorly run."

"You certainly wouldn't know it by looking at it now. I must say she did an excellent job of turning it around."

"Yes," Charles said, looking at her, "she did."

A smile would have been nice too, Becky thought, or even a thank-you for her compliment, but time was on her side. He was going to come around sooner or later. She was patient.

"You ladies get back to work," Charles said as he left the desk and headed toward Jenay's office.

Marla gave him a chilling look. "You heard him?" she asked Becky. "*You ladies get back to work*, he said. He doesn't have to tell us to get to work. We know to get back to work. But did you see it? Mean as a junkyard dog!"

Becky nodded, but she was equally curious to know just how good in bed that mean dog was.

Charles, unaware of her interest or Marla's distaste, and not caring either way, knocked one time and then entered Jenay's office. He began walking toward the desk. Jenay was seated behind her desk, and Donald was seated on the side chair. "Forty more at the front desk too?" he asked her.

"At least forty," Jenay said. "That part of the protocol is on us. We don't want to look as if we held back. We want more of these kind of balls. Tell them to go all out. Decorate that space as if they were spearheading the ball themselves."

"Yes, ma'am," Donald said as he stood up. "Hey, Dad," he added as he headed out. "Bye, Dad."

Charles didn't respond as Donald left. He, instead, made his way toward the desk. "Busy?" he asked Jenay as he plopped down on the chair in front of her desk.

Jenay noticed the strained look on his face. "Not really," she said. "What's up?"

Charles stretched out his legs and crossed them at the ankle. "What are you doing?"

"Just going over protocols. Nothing special. What's going on with you?"

There was a hesitation. "You saw the news reports?" he asked her.

"Of you throwing that guy off of the public sidewalk? Of you destroying his bullhorn?"

Charles stared at her. Would she judge him harshly too? "Yes."

"I saw it."

"And what did you think of it?"

"I thought he had it coming to him," Jenay said frankly. "They're there to create a commotion, that's the only reason they were there."

"And I played into it," Charles admitted.

"Yes, you did," Jenay said. "But I'll bet you one thing: those so-called protestors won't be coming back. They won't be creating any more commotions around your place of business."

Charles smiled. "That's true."

"It's not pretty how you do things, babe," Jenay said, and Charles looked at her. "But it's always effective," she added. "I'll take effectiveness over politeness any day of the week."

Charles felt that swell of emotion he often felt when Jenay demonstrated her love for him. This time her words said it all. "Thanks," he said with a weak smile.

But Jenay knew him too well. "But that's not what's really bothering you. Is it?"

Charles drew his legs back up and leaned forward in his chair. Most men with his vast business interests often had many advisors. Charles only had one: Jenay. He trusted her advice as profoundly as he trusted his own instincts. "They want to shut me down," he said.

"Shut you down?"

"That's what I'm thinking, yeah."

"But, Charlie, don't you think that's a little excessive? I mean, Cruikshank is running his mouth. But it seems like nothing more than a clown show to get elected. I never took it seriously."

But Charles did, and his facial expression told Jenay that he did. "So you think there's more to it than this election? Is that what you're telling me?"

"That's the way it's shaking out to me," Charles replied. "I looked into the eyes of that protestor this morning. That guy was no protestor. That guy's a professional thug. If those hidden cameras weren't rolling, he would have done a lot more than the little fighting back he called himself doing." He looked at his wife. "There's something more at work here, Jenay. I can feel it. I've felt it for some time now. Cruikshank may be the pawn, or he may be the mastermind. I don't know which. But they want to shut me down."

"But what's their motivation? So they can take over? Is that what you're saying?"

"Whoever *they* are," Charles said. "Yes. That's what I'm saying."

A worried look crossed Jenay's face. She was about to say more, but Tony walked in.

"Hello, parents," he said. "Look what the cat drug in?"

Tony was dressed down, in a pair of faded blue jeans, a sweat shirt, and tennis shoes. A lot of grease spots stained his shirt. "Drug is right," Jenay said, looking him up and down. "I know you didn't go to work looking like that."

"I work at a radio station, Jenay," Tony pointed out. "Who's going to see me?"

"The people who work with you at that station," Charles said.

Tony smiled, and plopped down on the chair beside his father. "No worries, people. This is my day off. I've been working on some of my cars."

"Don't tell me you bought another car," Charles said.

"Just this magnificent '66 Studebaker."

"Anthony! Not another one."

"But this one isn't like that other one. That other one was just a hunk of junk. This one has potential."

Charles and Jenay looked at each other and shook their heads.

"Okay, don't believe me. But you guys should stop judging me and come over to my place and take a look. It's a classic I'm telling you. And when I get it restored, man oh man. It's going to be a beauty to see."

"And you won't sell it, will you?"

"Not for all the tea in China," Tony admitted. "But it'll still be a beauty to see."

Knocks were heard on Jenay's door. Marla opened the door. "Excuse me, Mrs. Sinatra."

"Yes?"

"Carly is here with someone she wishes to introduce you to."

"Someone? Who?"

"The new head mistress at Saint Catherine's Preparatory Academy."

Tony smiled. "A woman running Saint Cat's? And those old biddies over there are going to let her run it?" He stood up. "This I've got to see."

"Thanks, Marla, I'll be right out," Jenay said. Marla left.

Jenay stood up too. "Wonder what that's about?" she asked. "I'm with Tony. I can't imagine that group hiring a woman."

Charles stood up too. He was just as curious as they were. Saint Catherine's was one of the oldest, and most conservative institutions in Jericho. This was rather shocking.

But when Charles, Jenay and Tony made their way out of the office and into the hotel's lobby, there was more than curiosity and shock that met their gaze. Carly was standing in the

middle of the lobby talking with the new head
mistress, a tall, African-American woman who
appeared to be in her late twenties. And each
one of them, on seeing her, had their own
reactions.

For Charles, it was her remarkable
presence. She was no beauty. She did not
have Jenay's good looks, or even Makayla's.
And if he was to be plain about it, she was, in
truth, most unattractive. Her face was too
long, her eyes were too far apart, and her skin,
with that so-called *high yellow* tone that was
generally thought beautiful, displayed a flush of
freckles across her cheekbones that made it
look ruddy.

But there was something about her that
was alluring too. It could have been her long,
wavy hair that dropped along her back in
waves of bounciness. Or it could have been
her slender frame. Jericho men, Charles not
included, tended to have a preference for
women with her body type. But Charles
doubted if her hair texture and body type were
her saving grace. He suspected it was her
bearing. She stood straight-backed, and had an
elegance about her, as if she was high-bred and
sophisticated and didn't care if you liked it or
not. She wasn't snooty as some ladies of her
class could be, but he could tell she had

confidence in spades. It was a presence that demanded respect, a commanding presence, that he saw in her.

Jenay saw it too. She saw it the way she carried herself. She saw it in what she was raised to refer to as *good* hair, although she hated the term. It made it sound as if natural, kinky hair wasn't good, when she knew that it was. But that long hair seemed to define her too somehow. And even her freckles set her apart. She was different, and it showed. Or maybe it was just the fact that a place like Saint Catherine's would hire a young woman like her was more the fascination for Jenay.

Tony, however, immediately discounted his fascination with her selection, as Jenay saw it, or even her unattractive looks and her presence, as his father saw it. Because as soon as Tony entered that lobby and saw Sharon standing there, a feeling came over him that was so profusely odd that it stopped him in his tracks. It went as fast as it came, like a quick wind out of nowhere, and he recovered. But as he finally followed his parents toward her, and as he realized Carly had already introduced their parents to her and explained the reason for her visit, he was still reeling by his initial response. What in the world, he wondered, was that about?

"How do you like Jericho so far?" Jenay was asking Sharon when Tony approached their circle.

"I haven't seen an awful lot of it," Sharon responded. "But so far so good."

Sharon felt more relaxed around Jenay. She would hope it wasn't simply because Jenay was black like her, but because Jenay had a sweet spirit about her that was contagious. She liked her. Carly, on the other hand, was smiling just as much as Jenay, and had a sweetness about her too, but Sharon sensed a foreboding in Carly. A depression. An inward terror that her smile could not tamp down.

"This knucklehead right here," Charles said when Tony finally arrived in the group, "is my second oldest son, Anthony. Anthony, meet Sharon Flannigan, the new principal at Saint Catherine's. She's going to be staying here at the Inn for a spell."

Tony extended his hand. "Nice to meet you," he said.

"And you," Sharon responded, shaking his hand. He was staring at her while they shook, and even before they shook, which was unusual. It had been her experience that men tended to view her as nothing special to look at, and she was accustomed to that reality. What could this son of Sinatra, a very handsome son at that, possibly find so fascinating?

"Tony's a radio star," Carly said proudly. "At least here in Jericho he is."

Sharon smiled. "Really? A star?"

"If you keep in mind that anybody on the radio in Jericho is a star, then yes, I'm a star."

Sharon laughed. "What are you starring in on the radio?"

"Therapy sessions."

"He's a clinical psychologist who gives people advice over the radio," Carly added.

"I see," Sharon said. She also wondered if Carly was availing herself of his advice. "Perhaps I'll phone in one day."

"When those old biddies at Saint Cat's get through with you," Tony said, reclaiming his upbeat personality, "you'll call."

Sharon laughed again, as did Charles, Jenay and Carly. For a stuffy old head mistress, Charles thought, she was alright. She so intrigued him that he had to ask her. "Speaking of old biddies," he said, "how did a nice girl like you end up in a place like Saint Cat's?"

"I was asked to come. Or, correction, ordered here. I was the dean of students at Saint Catherine's Prep Academy in Baltimore when my bishop asked if I would like to relocate to Maine."

"And I'm sure you told him it would be your pleasure," Jenay said sarcastically.

"I told him was he on dope?" Sharon said, and they all laughed. "I told him no, sir, I would not like to relocate to Maine." She exhaled. She was still smiling, but Tony could see the disappointment in her big, hazel eyes. "But he was firm. He needed me here."

"You could have quit," Carly said. "He couldn't force you to relocate."

"It's only temporary," Sharon said definitively.

Tony had a feeling she was wishfully thinking. "He told you that?" he asked.

"No, but if I complete my mission, if I turn things around as was his mandate to me, then I suspect I'll be back in Baltimore in no time."

That's what you think, Carly thought, as someone who knew just how dysfunctional the Academy truly was. But that was for Sharon to find out for herself.

"Are you married?" Tony asked. "Have any little babies running around?"

"No," Sharon said, looking at Tony. "I've never been married." Never been asked either, Tony suspected. "And, of course, I have no children."

"You speak as if marriage is a requirement for having children," Tony said. "It is not, I can tell you."

"It is for me," Sharon corrected him. "I can tell *you*."

Charles smiled. "The Irish ladies that I've known," he said, "aren't so black and white. They have babies out of wedlock all over the place. And you are Irish, right?"

Carly laughed. "Many black people have Irish surnames, Dad. That doesn't make them all Irish."

"Actually," Sharon said, "my father's father was half-Irish on his paternal side. Thus the name Flannigan."

"I see," Charles said, with a nod of the head.

"But in answer to your comment, I never base my way of life on how a particular group base theirs."

"Good answer," Tony said, and as soon as he said it, the sound of breaking glass could be heard.

Charles looked beyond Jenay, whose back was to the room-sized picture window inside the lobby, and saw the window shatter. He also saw what he thought was a rifle hanging out of a car stopped at the curb.

"*Get down!*" he shouted with a thunderous shout and pushed down both his wife and daughter, diving on top of both of them. Tony instinctively dived too, on top of Sharon, and covered her body with his. Just as they dived, that lone shot that shattered the window, took on more urgency and bullets ripped through the lobby window and hit walls and vases and flower pots and everything else in sight.

Both men covered the ladies as hails of bullets flew past them like sparks of fire. Marla and Becky, who were still behind the front desk counter when the gunfire erupted, dropped to the floor to, behind the counter, screaming in fear. The guests who were in the lobby dropped down screaming too. It was a moment of terror that nobody in that room would ever forget. Because of the sounds. Because of the unrelenting sounds of bullets bouncing off of walls, ricocheting and breaking other glassware, and echoing in their ears. Until, as Charles suspected would eventually happen, the gunman ran out of bullets to fire.

When Charles looked up, he could see the rifle moving back into the car, and the car burning rubber taking off.

He looked at Jenay and Carly, who were still lying down. "You two okay?" he asked them.

Carly nodded, and Jenay said that she was okay.

"Tony?" Charles yelled, as he hurriedly

stood up.

Tony, still lying on Sharon, nodded. "We're okay," he said.

Donald, who had been upstairs, ran down the stairs just as Charles took off running out of the lobby and onto the street. "What happened?" he was asking as he ran down those stairs.

But Charles was already gone. When Charles made it out onto the street, he saw the car driving fast and recklessly toward the end of the street. He did not hesitate. He pulled out the handgun he had only recently began carrying and took off on foot. He knew this town. He knew this street would dead-end on Lennox and that getaway car would have to go left, along Spirit, until he was at the stop sign on Cash and Spirit. There was only one way to turn there too.

Charles took off running across the street, through the back of the row houses, jumping the fence toward another set of row houses that led him onto Cash. But the car sped past him just as he was running onto Cash. The car was driving so fast that Charles didn't have time to fire his weapon. But he saw who it was. He stared at the driver as the car flew past. He saw that protestor. The one he encountered that morning. Abe Norris. He saw that motherfucker.

"Dad! Dad!"

He turned. It was Donald.

"Dad, come quick," Donald said.

"What is it?" Charles asked, even though he didn't hesitate. He began running toward his son.

"It's Mom, Dad," Donald said nervously as his father ran toward him.

Charles's heart began to hammer. "Jenay?"

"She didn't realize it," Donald said. "We didn't realize it!"

"Didn't realize what?" Charles asked anxiously. "What are you talking about?"

"She was hit," Donald said. "We didn't realize Mom had been shot!"

Charles's heart fell like a lump of hot coal through his entire body, and he took off. He ran with fire under his feet. He left his own son, who was younger and faster and smaller than him by a heap, in a trail of dust and tears.

CHAPTER TWELVE

"Yes, sir. No, sir. No, sir."

Brent paced the hospital waiting room fielding question after question from his boss, the mayor. He was talking on his cell phone and but for his conversation, the silence was deafening.

"No, sir. There were additional reports of injuries, but those were mostly from glass or somebody injured in a fall. Only one person was shot." Brent stopped walking and exhaled. "My stepmother," he said with pain in his voice.

Robert slid down the wall until he was crotched to the floor, his hands in his blond hair as he felt the sting all over again. He and Jenay were close. He never dreamed something like this would happen to her.

Ashley and Donald were also in the waiting room, sitting on the sofa side by side, still wiping tears from their eyes. Carly was sitting on the sofa too, but further over, and alone. Unlike Ash and Donald, she had not been crying. But her heart was racing.

In the back of the room, standing on either

side of the small window, was Tony, along with Sharon Flannigan. Both were silent, deep in their thoughts, and praying. Sharon had no intentions of coming to the hospital, but after Tony had saved her life (and he had when he dived on top of her), she couldn't just let him go alone. She somehow felt connected to him now. She somehow felt an obligation to make sure he was okay.

But when the waiting room door opened, and Charles walked in, Tony hurried to his father so fast, as did the rest of his siblings, until it forced Sharon to bring up the rear alone. Even Brent abruptly ended his call with the mayor to hear what his father had to say. And Sharon understood their anxiety. If it had been her mother, she would be anxious too. Besides, Mr. Sinatra, she felt, looked like a man on the verge of falling apart. He looked devastated. But his words to his children weren't.

"She's going to be okay," Charles quickly reassured his children.

Everybody let out a collective sigh of relief. "Thank God," Tony added.

"The doctor said the bullet only grazed her arm," Charles continued. "It's painful for her, very painful, but she'll be okay." Then he looked around. "Where's Bonita?"

"With Makayla and Junior," Brent said. "She's in good hands."

Charles nodded, and then wiped across his eyes with the back of his hand. He was exhausted. "Good," he said.

"But who would do this to Mom?" Ashley asked, wiping away tears. "She wouldn't harm a flea! Who would do this to her?"

"Who says it was Mom they were doing it to?" Donald asked. "She's been standing in that lobby every day for years, and nobody's shot at her until today. And the only reason she was standing there today was because she was being introduced to that lady over there." Donald pointed at Sharon. "She's the only person here who's never been at the Inn before. She's the only person here who's never been in Jericho before. Maybe she was the one they were after, and Mom got in the way."

Normally, Brent wouldn't give Donald's wild assertions a second thought. He was always pointing fingers at somebody but himself. But this time he couldn't so easily dismiss the claim. Because Donald was right. Sharon Flannigan was the only unknown quantity who was standing where the gunman's bullets had targeted.

Tony, however, was completely dismissive.

"That's utter nonsense!" he fired back. "Sharon Flannigan had nothing more to do with some crazed gunman deciding to shoot up the place than me or you or Carly over there. She was in the wrong place at the wrong time. Full stop. Period."

"And how do you know that?" Donald asked. "You just met the woman, Tone. How would you know anything about her?"

"She was not the target," Tony said with a kind of unwavering confidence even he knew was absurd. "You're barking up the wrong tree."

"Oh, so I'm a dog now?" Donald asked.

"Knock it off," Brent said with a frown. It was stressful enough. Then he exhaled. And looked at Sharon. "May I have a word?" he asked her.

Tony frowned himself. "Brent!"

"I have to do my job, Tony. I'm police chief in this county and a shooting has occurred. I have to question her."

"You're going to listen to Donnie's ridiculousness?"

"It's not ridiculous," Donald said. "It's facts. And what's your problem anyway? What are you defending her for? She's not even cute!"

Tony moved to rearrange his kid brother's

146

face, but Brent stood in the way. "I told you two to knock it off!"

"It's alright," Sharon said, looking flustered too. Then she looked at Brent. "Yes, you may question me," she said.

Brent looked at Tony. Tony finally backed off. After he did, Brent and Sharon walked back over to the window in the back of the room. Tony glared at Donald, but then followed them.

But the rest of the Sinatra clan was less interested in who did it, than their mother's wellbeing. "When can we see her, Dad?" Carly asked their father. "Can we see her now?"

"She's asleep, but you can see her," Charles said, and they hurried toward the door. "Don't wake her," he yelled after them, "or I'll kick all of your asses!"

"Yes, sir," Carly yelled back, as she, Robert, Donald and Ashley hurried out of the door. Charles looked over at Brent as he prepared to question Sharon. But he already knew who did it. The question for him was why. Before Brent got involved and slowed the process as law enforcement always did, he had to find out for himself.

As Brent and Sharon talked, and as Tony paid attention to that conversation, Charles eased out of the waiting room, and then the hospital altogether. He had places to go. A person to see. That damned protestor shot his wife. He had to find out why. He had to find out what the hell was going on once and for all, before any more of his loved ones were harmed.

Brent didn't realize his father had even left the room as he questioned Sharon. She told him why she was in Jericho, and why she was at the Jericho Inn. But Brent needed more.

"The shooting occurred less than an hour after you arrived in town." Brent waited for her to agree with him. But she didn't. She wasn't going to participate in her own lynching. So he continued. "Before you arrived, was there anybody you can recall who might have some beef with you? Some grudge?"

"No one," she said quickly.

Too quick for Brent. "Shouldn't you give it some thought before you answer?" he asked her.

"I have already given it thought," Sharon responded. "Considerable thought. There is no one."

"Look Miss Flannigan," Brent said, "it's my job to find out if you were involved in this shooting or not. I'm not trying to give you a hard time."

"Insinuating that I brought this trouble to

Jericho is my idea of a hard time," Sharon shot back.

"You don't have to take it personally."

"Oh, Brent, give me a break!" Tony said. "How else is she supposed to take it? As a group? Of course it's personal. And she's right. You can't lay this mess at her feet."

Brent ignored Tony. He was always taking on crusades, and apparently this school teacher was his new pet project. But Brent still had a job to do. "Maybe your ex-boyfriend," he said to Sharon, "could hold some grudge. Or an ex-husband?"

Tony could see a sadness suddenly appear in her eyes. "No," she said. "There's no one that I'm aware of who would have ever perpetrated this crime. I'm sorry, Chief, but I cannot help you. Am I excused?"

"After you answer my questions, yes. Is there an ex-boyfriend or ex-husband or whomever out there who may wish to do you harm?"

"No," Sharon said firmly. "There is no ex-boyfriend. There is no ex-husband. I cannot help you, Chief. Am I excused?"

Tony looked at Sharon. Brent thought she meant there were no ex who wished to do her harm. But he could see the pain in her eyes. There were no ex period. No prior relationship period. And it was a painful part of what had to be her lonely existence. His heart, once again, went out to her and he couldn't understood why. She was an accomplished woman. She didn't need his sympathy or empathy or even his concern. But to Tony's own astonishment, she had all three.

Brent, giving up, nodded. "Yes, you're excused," he said. "I apologize if I offended you, Miss Flannigan, but I have a job to do."

"I fully understand," she said. And as Brent left to go check on Jenay too, she looked at Tony. "I'm glad your stepmother is doing better. I'm very pleased with the news. But I'm going to leave."

"If you can wait a few moments for me to at least eyeball my mother for myself," Tony said, "then I'll be happy to take you back to the Inn. Or wherever you want to go. You rode with me, and the least I can do is drive you back." When she appeared to be wary of waiting, he went a step further. "Please," he added.

Sharon really didn't see why she couldn't just call a cab and leave, but she nodded.

And Tony hurried out of the waiting room. But when he eyeballed Jenay for himself, and saw that she was medicated and resting comfortably as his father had said, he hurried back into the waiting room. But it was no surprise to him that Sharon had gone.

Jeff Cruikshank heard the commotion, but turned too late. Charles grabbed him by the catch of his collar and flung him against the wall.

"What's the meaning of this?" Cruikshank asked. "What are you doing, Sinatra?"

"What game are you playing at?" Charles angrily asked. "What the fuck is this about?!"

Cruikshank's campaign volunteers ran into his office, but stopped in their tracks when they saw the perpetrator was Big Daddy. They knew how mean, and powerful, he was.

"I don't know what you're talking about!" Cruikshank insisted.

"Where is he?"

"What are you talking about?"

"Where is that fucker that tried to kill my wife?" Then Charles slammed him against the wall again. "Where is he, *got*dammit?!"

"I don't know. Get him off of me! I don't know what you're talking about!"

"They wanted me, but they got my wife. My wife!" Charles said with anger and pain in his voice. Then he pulled out his gun, and put it to Cruikshank's head. The volunteers took off running out of the office. "Nobody threatens my wife and get away with it. That's not going to happen."

"But it's not true, man!" Cruikshank cried. "I didn't order anybody to do anything to you or your wife! I didn't do it!"

The volunteers nearly ran Brent over as he hurried into the storefront building. "He's got a gun!" one volunteer was screaming as he ran out. "Big Daddy's got a gun!"

Brent ran into the building, pushed past the last of the volunteers who were running out, and hurried to the back office where he saw Cruikshank and his father. "Dad, you can't," he said anxiously. "Don't do it!"

Charles heard Brent's voice.

"Dad, don't," Brent said again, and walked over to his father.

"Tell him I'm innocent," Cruikshank said. "Tell him I had nothing to do with his wife's shooting. Tell him, Brent!"

Brent, ignoring Cruikshank, attempted to ease the gun out of his father's hand. Charles would not relinquish his weapon. Nobody dictated to him, least of which his own son. But he did remove the gun from Cruikshank's head.

"I don't know what you're talking about," Cruikshank said again. "I had nothing to do with your wife's shooting."

"Where's Norris?" Charles asked.

"I don't know him. I told the press I don't know him! People have been claiming he works for me, but he doesn't. The news media have been spreading those lies. I've never met the man before, and I don't know anything about him. I swear. I don't know him! Nobody in my campaign knows him! I'm not guilty, Big Daddy!"

Charles stared at Cruikshank. The fact that he was pleading innocence only made matters worse. Now he didn't have a clue why Norris harmed Jenay. But he released him. Cruikshank could be lying, but somehow he doubted it.

Charles put his gun away, left the small, storefront campaign building and stepped out onto the sidewalk. Cruikshank began complaining to Brent that Charles should be arrested for attempting to murder him, but Brent warned that he would sic his father back on him if he didn't cut that foolish talk out. Cruikshank cut it out.

When Brent got outside, Charles was just standing there, thinking. "What's going on, Dad?" Brent asked. "Why would you think Jeff Cruikshank had something to do with Mom's shooting?"

"I saw the gunman," Charles said.

Brent was floored. "You saw him? And didn't tell me?"

"I saw Norris," Charles said.

"Who?"

"Abe Norris. That protestor."

"The one you roughed up this morning?" Brent asked.

Charles nodded. "He was the shooter," he said. "I ran after the car, and I saw him behind the wheel."

Brent ran his hand through his head. "Why didn't you tell me, Dad?"

"Because I need to know what's going on! I assumed he worked for Cruikshank. The press said he worked for Cruikshank."

"But Cruikshank's saying something totally different," said Brent.

Charles exhaled. "I know that. But something's going on here. And it isn't random, and it isn't accidental. I don't want to hear that shit. Not after they harmed Jenay. Something is at work here. Before another member of my family is harmed, or those fuckers try it again with my wife, I've got to find out what."

Brent nodded. "I'll put a BOLO, a *be on the lookout*, on Abe Norris. But you've got to let me handle this, Dad. We'll find him, and we'll get to the bottom of this. But the legal way."

Charles nodded his agreement. And he began walking away.

"Where are you going now?" Brent asked.

"Back to the hospital," Charles said. "To be with my wife."

Brent exhaled, and watched him leave.

"Hope I didn't disturb you," Tony asked when Sharon opened the door of her room at the Inn.

"I was reading," Sharon said as if it was a disturbance. She had a book in her hand.

"Reading what?" Tony asked.

"Re-familiarizing myself with some liturgy. As Head Mistress of the church school, I have to make sure the staff and students adhere to certain protocol."

"So you were reviewing what? *The Book of Common Prayer*?"

"Exactly. Of course its formal name," she added, "is far more extensive."

"*The Book of Common Prayer*," said Tony, "*and Administration of the Sacraments and Other Rites and Ceremonies of the Church Together with The Psalter or Psalms of David According to the use of The Episcopal Church*."

Sharon was surprised.

"In my prior life," Tony said, "I studied theology too."

Sharon smiled. "Good for you."

"Why did you leave?" Tony asked, as if he was getting to the real reason for his visit.

Sharon didn't want this visit. She didn't want this exposure. She didn't want to befriend him or anybody else at this time in her life. She just wanted to be left alone. "I have a full day ahead of me tomorrow," she said. "The rector gave me the rest of the day off. I needed to take full advantage of it."

Tony understood that. "Certainly," he said with a nod of the head. "It's not the first day of work you had envisioned, I'm sure."

Sharon smiled warily. "Not hardly," she said. "How's your stepmother?" she asked.

"She's okay. Sleeping. Resting. She'll pull through just fine."

"Your father seemed really upset."

Tony nodded. "He loves her. He loves us all. But he loves her."

Sharon didn't detect any resentment in his voice.

"Look, I won't keep you," Tony said. "I know you need some rest yourself. But I did want to apologize for my brother. He had no call questioning you like that."

"It was okay," she said. "He doesn't know me."

"I don't know you either," Tony admitted,

"but . . ."

Sharon stared at him. "But what?" she asked.

"But somehow it seems as if I know all about you," Tony said.

Sharon smiled. "So I'm not the only one?"

Tony was surprised. And then he smiled too. But then his smile left, and he turned serious. "No," he said. "You aren't the only one." Then he exhaled. "I'll let you get your rest. Goodbye, Sharon."

"Goodnight," Sharon responded. And closed the door. But as soon as she did, tears welled up in her eyes. Did his brother know? Did that police chief have the goods on her? Was this town going to turn on her too?

She was swimming. At least he thought she was. She started out swimming. But then he saw her arms, and they weren't stroking as he thought, but flailing. And she wasn't laughing, but crying. She was crying for help.

Trevor jumped out of his lounger on the beach, flipped off his flip flops, ran into the water and then dived in. He stroked his way to where she was flailing, and reached for her. But she wasn't there. He came up for breath, with his brown hair matted against his face, as he dived back in and stroked and searched for her. But he didn't see her. Then he came back up for breath, and saw her again.

"Mr. Reese," she cried. "*Mr. Reese*!"

She wasn't flailing anymore, but going down. Way down. She was drowning. Trevor dove in again, to rescue her, but he didn't see her beneath. He searched and searched, but there was no sign of her. He came back up for air, and didn't see her at all!

"*Carly*!" he cried. "*Carly*!" He dived back in again. Came back up again. "Carly! Carly!" But no sight of her. And when he turned around, and around some more, he realized he wasn't a few feet from shore as he had thought, but was in the middle of the ocean. And he was all alone the way Carly was, and now drowning too.

When he felt a tug, and went under, he woke up with a hard lift up. He realized then that he was not in the middle of the Atlantic Ocean, but was in his bed in Boston. And although Carly wasn't drowning, she was still alone.

He laid back down, drenched in sweat.

CHAPTER THIRTEEN

Two Weeks Later

"I'm not a baby, Charles."

"I didn't say you were. But you need to give yourself time to heal, Jenay. You need to give it more time."

"I gave it more time. The doctor said I could resume my normal activities within a couple of days after he released me from that hospital. The only reason I didn't go back to work when he said I could is because of you. But I'm fine, honey. I'll go stir crazy if I have to stay cooped-up in this house another day."

They were in their bedroom at home. Charles, never a morning person, was still in bed, lying on his back. Jenay was sitting at her dressing table, fresh out of the shower but had put back on her bathrobe. She was hot curling her hair.

Charles let out a tough exhale. Jenay looked at him through her dressing table mirror. "Everything's fine, Charlie."

"Yeah, well," Charles said as if he wasn't at all convinced, "somebody harms my wife and two weeks later they still don't have him in custody. That's not my idea of everything being fine."

"Brent's men have no clue where that protestor might be?" she asked.

"They don't even know who he is. He claimed his name was Abe Norris, but that was just some name he made up. It's not his real name. And other than that, nobody knows a damn thing. Maybe if I wasn't so certain it was Cruikshank, I could have told Brent sooner. Maybe they would have been able to track that asshole down that same day. But I was convinced Cruikshank was behind it, and he would give up, not only the guy, but the reason for his vendetta against me in the first place."

"What did Cruikshank tell you?"

"He told me nothing. He knows nothing. There's no vendetta, he claims. It's all politics. He told me nothing."

"They'll find him, Charles," Jenay said firmly. "Brent's good at his job."

But Charles knew Brent was a small-town police chief with the resources of a small-town police chief. "What Brent doesn't know is that I've hired private investigators to work this case too."

Jenay looked at him. "Private investigators?"

"That's right. Five different ones. But they haven't turned up shit either. I'm wasting my money."

Jenay could feel his frustration. "It'll work out," she said to him.

Charles knew she didn't need this extra aggravation, so he attempted to minimize his own anxiety. "I'm sure it will," he said.

Jenay smiled, and refocused on her grooming. When she finished curling her hair, she stood up to head to their room-sized closet. But Charles tossed the bedding off of him. "Let me take a look at the bandage," he said.

Jenay had already changed it, and it was fine. But Charles always had to see it for himself. She walked over to him as he flung his legs out and sat on the edge of the bed. He was naked, but Jenay wasn't exactly dressed either.

She stood between his legs as he untied her robe, revealing her nakedness. She then removed one arm out of the arm of the robe. An ace bandage covered her small bicep.

"How does it feel?" he asked as he checked for leakage.

"It feels okay. Most times I don't even remember that I have an injury. It hasn't been a problem."

Then Charles's eyes glanced down, at her flat stomach, at her taut brown breasts, and then he looked into her eyes. "And what about you?" he asked. "How are you feeling?"

Jenay smiled. "I'm glad to be getting back to work. Donnie's running the place in my absence, and I hear he's doing a good job, but I'm ready to get back."

"I can't understand that boy of mine," Charles said. "Sometimes he'll rise to the occasion in remarkable ways, and then other times he won't rise at all. I wonder if he'll ever be consistent, and which Donald will he ultimately become."

"You mean will he consistently be *good* Donald, or consistently be *bad* Donald?"

"He can go either way," Charles said with a smile, "as you have found out for yourself."

"And how," Jenay said with a smile of her own as she removed her robe completely. "I have the invisible scars to prove it." She tossed her robe onto the bed, and headed for her lingerie drawer.

But when she began walking away from Charles, and he watched as the cheeks of her smooth brown ass moved up and down with every stepdown, tight as hell, his cock began to throb. It had been two weeks, the morning before the shooting, since he last fucked her. "Jenay?"

She glanced back.

"Come here," he said.

When she saw his erection, she shook her head. She knew what he wanted. But now? "Come on, Charles."

But Charles was not relenting. "Don't *come on, Charles* me. Come here."

Jenay reluctantly walked back to the bed. Not because she didn't want to be with him. She always wanted it. But she didn't think her heart would be in it. She was still too focused on how she was going to react when she walked into the Inn for the first time since the shooting to even begin to experience any horniness.

Charles had already picked up on her anxiety. That was why, when she walked back up to him, he opened his legs wider, pulled her closer and into his arms, and reassured her even as he kissed and sucked her breasts. "You're going to be alright, babe," he said as he sucked her. "I'll make sure of that."

Jenay leaned her head back as he sucked her, but the reality of her situation was still front and center in her mind. "It'll be my first time back since the shooting," she said. "I'm worried about my reaction."

Charles looked at her. Jenay was a strong woman. When she admitted a concern so plainly, he knew it was a major concern for her. "Don't worry," he said. "I'll go with you. I'll rearrange my schedule and spend the entire day with you. If you feel any way threatened or anxious or anything like that, I'll bring you back home. And tomorrow we'll try again. And the day after that. Until you're okay."

Jenay stared at him. No human being alive had ever treated her the way Charles treated her. Then she smiled. "I thought you said I wasn't ready to go back to work," she teased. "Now you not only accept the fact that I'm going back, you're offering to go with me? That's a twist."

"That's love," Charles said as he turned her around, where her back was to his face, and sat her on his lap. Or more specifically, he sat her on his penis. "You give me what I need," he said as he lifted her small legs over his massive thighs and began rubbing her pussy. "And I give you what you need."

Jenay was enjoying his massage. "You think you know what I need?" she asked him.

He began to rub harder. He began to breathe harder into her ear. "I think I do."

"Oh, yeah?" she asked, her own breathe becoming labored. "And what's that?"

"This," Charles said as he thrust two digits deep inside of her and with his thumb began to flick her clit. Only he flicked it with such ferocity that Jenay's body began to jerk in reaction.

"Like it?" Charles said as he flicked her faster and faster, and dug his fingers in deeper and deeper in simulation of a penis.

"I like it," Jenay said.

"Like this?" Charles asked, as he continued to watch her and do her.

"Like that," Jenay said breathlessly as he kept doing her and doing her until she was on the verge of cum.

He was studying her. He knew she was near. "Ready to cum, baby?"

"I'm ready," Jenay said.

"Almost there?" Charles asked, doing her even harder.

"Almost," Jenay said in a voice barely audible.

Then Charles lifted his fully erected penis, thrust it inside of her super-wet pussy, and began to fuck her at the apex of her cum.

Her orgasm started within seconds of his entry. And by the time he was in full rhythm, stroking her with fast, brutal, unrelenting thrusts, she was jerking and tightening and pulsating until her toes curled.

Charles laid back on the bed, lifted her legs, and fucked her even harder. He went down so deep inside of her that his balls were trying to get in too. They slapped against the outer reaches of her pussy as his rod slammed into the inner reaches. And when he ejaculated inside of her, his cum was almost watery as it began to fly out of her like drops of rain spewing out. And then it was white, and thick, and began to slide out of her vagina, down his penis, like cream.

He pushed into her for the final push, made a grunting noise that almost sounded like an animal, and then slowly pulled out. Jenay felt every vein in his rob, and Charles felt every ridge of her pussy, as he continued to slowly pull out. She was still pulsating, and was covered with the level of cream pie that only overdue sex could produce, when he finally made it completely out.

Carly looked up from grading papers when the doorbell began ringing. She knew Donald was downstairs, so she didn't bother to answer. Like Carly, Donald moved back in with their parents too. But unlike Carly's situation, Donald moved back in after Charles and Jenay demoted him from the Inn's General Manager to desk clerk supervisor. But both were there to get back on their feet.

But when he yelled upstairs that the visitor wanted to see her, she frowned. Looked at her watch. It was just past seven in the morning.

Who in the world would be visiting her at this hour?

She hadn't even dressed for work yet, since she didn't have to be there until nine, and wore only a pair of Puma shorts and a Patriots t-shirt. But she placed her paperwork aside, got up from her bedroom desk, and made her way downstairs.

"Who is it?" she asked Donald as she headed for the living room. When she turned the corner and saw Donald standing there talking, she assumed it was somebody he knew too. But she was wrong.

"There she is," Donald said to whomever he was talking to. "It's one of your co-workers from Boston," he added to Carly with a smile.

When he moved aside, and Carly saw who he meant, she nearly died where she stood. Coworker her ass. It was her former boss! "It's you?" she asked, stunned witless. "*Mr. Reese*?"

Trevor Reese stood in her parents' living room. He stood with his long hair pulled back, his tailored suit buttoned and snug, and his big, violet eyes as sincere as a hawk's. "Hello, Carly," he said, and although her heart was hammering, he said it without a hint of emotion.

CHAPTER FOURTEEN

"I'm out," Donald said as he began heading for the front door.

"It's only seven a.m.," Carly said. She and Donald didn't get along on their best day. But she needed him by her side this day. "Where are you going this early?"

"I have Gilda's ride. I have to drop her off at work before I head to the Inn."

Gilda was Donald's biker chick girlfriend. "You don't know how to ride a motorcycle," Carly reminded him.

"Gill taught me, for your information," Donald said. "I'm out." He said his goodbyes to Trevor, and left Carly without hesitation.

"Your roommate?" Trevor asked in a voice that belied something more.

"My roommate?" Carly asked as if the mere idea was disagreeable. "No." Then she motioned for him to have a seat on the sofa.

"After you," Trevor said, and Carly sat down first. Trevor unbuttoned his suit coat, and took a seat too.

"So, Mr. Reese," Carly said with a nervous smile, "what in the world brings you to Jericho?

I didn't think you had any clients this far north."

"Actually, I do," Trevor responded. "I'm on my way to Montreal. But I wanted to drop by and see you first."

Carly's heart began to pound. She used to dream of him dropping by her house, to see her, to visit with her. But it never happened. "Why would you want to see me?"

Trevor stared at Carly. She was accustomed to his stares, as he always seemed to study her rather than look at her. But this stare seemed laced with something unfamiliar. Something she had never seen before. "I would think it is obvious, Carly," he said.

Carly didn't understand what he meant. "Obvious, sir? How so?"

Trevor continued to stare at her.

"Sir?" she asked.

"If he's not your roommate," Trevor asked, "then who is he?"

Carly was at first thrown. Why was he still harping on Donald? "He's my brother," she said.

"Oh," Trevor said in a voice that was flat, and didn't reveal any relief. "I see."

Her relationship with Donald, however, was the last thing on Carly's mind. "But why is your visit here obvious, sir?" she asked.

Trevor realized he had veered off course. "You left my employ so abruptly," he said.

"Abruptly?" Carly responded too quickly, and in a voice she knew was too defensive. "I gave two weeks' notice. Now was that abrupt, sir?"

"The timing, my dear, was then and is still now quite curious to me. I felt as if something more was going on."

Carly summoned all of her gifts of persuasion to counter what she was beginning to believe was his suspiciousness. "I don't know what you mean. My family was having difficulties, so I decided to move back home. The only thing that was going on, as you call it, was my desire to be with my family. I don't understand where you're going with this?"

Trevor smiled. "You know where I'm going," he said. "You just don't like that I'm going there."

The sound of footsteps on the stairs saved Carly's reaction. Instead of displaying the shock that was deep within her, she turned toward the sound. When her parents came around the archway, she didn't feel totally out of the woods, but she at least felt a temporary rescue. "Mom, Dad, hi."

Trevor immediately rose to his feet. The two people, well-dressed in their business suits, were hardly what he expected when he envisioned Carly's parents. The woman was a beautiful black woman, just as attractive as Carly herself, and Carly, to Trevor, was most attractive. But beyond beauty, they had nothing in common. Not even a little bit. And as to the muscular white man that she just so cavalierly referred to as her father, it wasn't even close. They didn't look at all alike. But races intermingled so much now, that it was hard to tell who was who anymore. "I'm Trevor Reese," he said, as he extended his hand. "It's very nice to meet you."

"Very nice to meet you, too," Jenay said as she shook his hand.

Charles shook his hand, too, but he was a little more hesitant. "Trevor Reese," he said. "That name sounds familiar."

Carly swallowed hard. Jenay could see the strain on her face. "He's my former boss, Dad."

Charles and Jenay both looked at their daughter. "Your former boss?" Charles asked.

"Yes," Trevor interjected. "While she lived in the Commonwealth, she ran my PR department. Ran it quite well, actually."

Jenay was beginning to smell a rat. Charles too. "And you're here why exactly?" he asked.

"I was worried about your daughter. I wanted to make sure she was okay."

Both Charles and Jenay knew something wasn't right when they saw this attractive man sitting in their living room. Carly had turned down more men than they could count since her return to Jericho. They assumed, after what happened in Boston, it was still too soon. But now that they knew Trevor was her former boss, their curiosity turned into downright concern.

"Perhaps I'm missing something," Charles said, "but why would you be worried about my daughter? Why wouldn't she be okay?"

"Just before she resigned," Trevor said, "one of our biggest clients, Ethan Campbell, went missing. He remains missing to this day. I didn't want the same fate to befall her."

All three Sinatras began to experience varying degrees of anxiety. The idea that he would mention Ethan, and the fact that he was missing, set it off.

"I don't understand," Charles said. "That kind of reasoning makes no sense to me. I'm sorry to hear about your client's fate, but why would you even suggest that Carly could have suffered the same?"

"Just the way I think," said Trevor. "I think circularly. I think there are no such things as coincidences and if my client goes missing and my best employee suddenly has a family emergency where she has to give notice and resign from her job, I make sure all is kosher."

"It's been nearly two months since she left your employ," Jenay said.

"I would have come sooner, but dealing with the disappearance of one of my biggest clients has been a twenty-four hour job. Especially since my PR department still has not recovered from Carly's absence. Yes, she was *that* good. And then I had other emergencies with other clients that prevented any inquiries. When I knew I was heading to Canada where one of my clients finds himself in a bit of a mess, I decided to do a spot check on my former employee. It's as simple as that."

Jenay didn't believe him. There was much more at work here. But she knew the best way to handle it, was to minimize it. "Well, we certainly appreciate your interest, Mr. Reese. It's very thoughtful of you to drop by."

Trevor smiled. "No problem at all. I'm just glad to see that all is well." Then he looked at Carly. "And I take it you're enjoying your new life here, and your teaching job?"

Carly fought hard against exposing her anxiety. "Yes," she said with a smile. "Very much so."

"Good." His big, violet eyes looked her up and down. Assessing her again. "Well. I won't keep you. As I said, I was headed to Canada and I need to get on with it. Have a good day."

Carly smiled. "Thank you," she said.

Trevor said his goodbyes to Charles and Jenay, and left.

After they saw him drive away, in a limousine of all vehicles, Charles and Jenay looked at Carly. "He knows," she said.

"Or maybe he just likes you," Charles said.

But Carly would have none of that. "No. No way. He never showed any interest in me whatsoever when we were within feet of each other every single day. But he's interested now? I don't buy it."

"Neither do I," Jenay said.

"Besides," Carly added, "he knew I was a teacher."

Charles and Jenay looked at her. "So?" Jenay asked.

"I never told him what I was doing, Ma. I never told him I was working at Saint Cat's. Why would he know that?"

Jenay already had her suspicions. That info just sealed it. But she didn't want to worry Carly. "He could have asked," she said.

"It's possible," Charles responded. "But I'm with Car. He didn't drop by here for the hell of it. She no longer works for him. Why should he care how she's doing? That man is up to something." Charles pulled out his cell phone.

"You think his presence here is related to the shooting at the Inn?" Jenay asked.

"I don't know," Charles said. "But I'm going to find out."

Brent was at the kitchen table with his wife Makayla when his cell phone rang. Brent looked at the Caller ID.

"Who is it?" Makayla asked.

"Dad," Brent said and answered. "Good morning."

"Any news on Abe Norris or whatever the hell his name is?"

"Not a word," Brent responded. "And we still don't know his real name."

"Listen, Brent," Charles said. "I want you to check Boston. See if you can find a connection between a guy who goes by Abe Norris's name, and Trevor Reese."

Brent frowned. "Who's Trevor Reese?"

"Carly's former boss who just so happens to have dropped by the house this morning. He claims to be worried about her."

Brent's heartbeat began to quicken. "You don't think?"

"I don't know," Charles said. "But it smells. Check him out. See if there's a connection."

Brent nodded. "Will do," he said.

"Call me when you find something," Charles said, and ended the call.

Makayla was the district attorney for Jericho County. She was a voluptuous black woman, smart and well-respected for her no-nonsense approach to her job. But Brent, who did not keep secrets from his wife, had told her about what happened with Ethan Campbell. She, too, knew about that unfortunate night. "What is it?" she asked as she stood and began to clear the table.

Brent looked at her. "Boston," he said.

Makayla stopped all activity. She knew exactly what he was talking about.

But Brent explained. She was his sounding board. "Carly's former boss," he said, "decided, out of the blue, to drop by and check on her."

"Were they close like that?"

"Dad didn't say, but it didn't sound like it. He wants me to see if there's a connection between that protestor and her boss."

"And what if there is a connection?" she asked.

Brent ran his hand through his thick, black hair. "Then somebody knows something," he said. "Then we're screwed," he added, as he looked her dead in the eyes.

And Makayla, fully understanding what that night could cost them, sat back down.

The connection could not have been more plausible moments later when knocks were heard on the Sinatras' front door. Charles answered, but Jenay and Carly were right there too. They were a well-known family, but even they didn't get this many guests this early in the morning. Especially, when Charles looked through the peephole and saw two very formal looking men, and a uniformed cop. He quickly opened the door. "Yes?" he asked. "May I help you?"

"Is Carly Sinatra here?" the man asked.

Carly stepped in front. "Yes?"

"Miss Sinatra, my name is Special Agent Goosley." He showed his ID. "This is Special Agent Javier Lucentos. And this is Officer Holland of the Jericho County Police Department. We need you to come with us, ma'am."

Charles moved back in front of his daughter. "Come with you where?"

"We're taking her back to Boston."

Carly felt faint. Was this really happening? "Why?" she asked as she moved beside her father. "May I ask why?"

"We have a warrant for your arrest,

ma'am," Goosley said. "We have extradition papers. We're here to take you back."

Jenay placed a hand around Carly's waist. "But what are you arresting her for?" she asked, reeling too.

"What's the charge?" Charles added.

"We have a warrant to arrest Carly Sinatra," Goosley said, "for the kidnapping and murder of Ethan Marvin Campbell."

They knew that had to be the reason, but just hearing those words still hit them like a ton of bricks. Because it was true. Because this wasn't just some miscarriage of justice, and they were all involved.

But Charles was not about to surrender not even a part of the point. "My daughter didn't murder or kidnap anybody," he said, as he pulled Carly back and stepped in front of her.

"Out of the way, sir." The agents placed their hands on their weapons. "Do not interfere with the performance of our responsibility or you will be arrested too."

"But what are you talking about?" Charles asked. "My daughter didn't kidnap and murder anybody!"

"Please step out, Miss Sinatra," Goosley said.

Carly was floored. "But I don't understand. Ethan is missing. They said he's missing. You found him?"

"We found his body," the agent said.

Charles knew better than that. He went with Mick to bury that body. He saw it with his own two eyes! "What does your finding his body have to do with my child?" he asked.

"What does it have to do with me?" Carly also asked.

"We found his body," Goosley said to her, "in the home in Boston that you, up until a few months ago, rented." He pulled Carly out of the house and began handcuffing her. "That's what it has to do with you."

Carly's heart was hammering. Jenay was so beside herself that she leaned against Charles to remain standing up. Charles put his arm around her, flustered too. Because it couldn't be possible. What were they talking about? They found the body in Carly's house? Ethan Campbell's body? In *Carly's* house? They didn't know what they were talking about!

But he knew there was nothing he could do at this point. Railing against the FBI was liking railing against the wind. They had no choice but to take the blows.

But Charles wasn't so thrown that he couldn't warn his daughter. "Don't you say a word to anybody," he ordered Carly as they followed her to a waiting patrol car. "They'll twist your words around and claim you confessed. Don't you say one word to anybody! You hear me, Carly?"

"Yes, sir," Carly said, as a pool of tears appeared in her big, sad eyes.

Charles's heart broke. "We'll get you out of this, baby," he said. "I'll get you out of this!"

But it was just talk and bluster, and they all knew it, as he and Jenay watched in horror as those law enforcement officers, those enforcers of laws they clearly had broken, took Carly away.

CHAPTER FIFTEEN

Somebody was blowing up his phone. Calling over and over again. He was in the back of his estate working out in his gym. He didn't have any of his men on any call-outs. Roz and the twins were up at the house. Nothing should have been this urgent. But he nodded to his spotter anyway. The spotter, a longtime employee, went over to the bench and grabbed his cell phone. Mick Sinatra lifted the weights up over his sweat-filled, muscular chest, and racked them.

He sat up and grabbed the towel. His spotter handed him the phone. "Who is it?" he asked.

"A Charles Sinatra, sir," the spotter replied. "According to the Caller ID."

Charles blowing up his phone like that? He was more curious now. His brother didn't call him unless it was serious. He took the phone from his spotter and answered it. "Good morning."

"They arrested her, Mick."

Mick knew who he meant. He could also detect terror in his brother's voice. "The police?"

"The FBI."

Mick's heartbeat began to quicken. It was always far more complicated when the Feds were involved. "Did they give a reason?"

"They said they found Campbell's body."

Mick frowned. "That is not possible."

"They said they found his body in the house she rented, Mick. They found his body in that fucking house!"

But Mick knew that couldn't be. "It wasn't left in the house. What are you saying? We moved it!"

"I know we moved it!" Charles yelled, his voice on the verge of hysterics. "I was there! I know we moved it!"

Mick knew there had to be something else going on. Were the Feds shitting with her to get her to talk? Or were they trying to out him, or Charles, or all of them? "Where are you now?" he asked his big brother.

"On my way to Boston. They're transporting her to the Boston jail now."

"When you arrive in Boston, do not go to the jail," Mick said. "Go to the airstrip and wait for me. I'm on my way."

"Brent and Makayla's on their way there now. So I guess I can do that."

"And Charles," Mick added, "make certain

you are not being followed."

There was an exasperated exhale over the phone. Mick knew Charles, a law and order man his whole life, hated to be on the wrong side of the law. But he'd go through fire for his children. Mick knew it now.

"I'll be careful," Charles responded. "You just get here." And then he ended the call.

Mick let out his own exhale when the call ended.

"The Feds on your case, boss?" the spotter asked.

Mick looked at him as if he had lost his mind. His spotter, suddenly realizing his error too, began moving back. But it was too late. Mick took the barbells he had been lifting and threw them at the man, knocking him down with a force that took his breath away. "Don't you ever question me about my own fucking business!" Mick yelled. "Not now. Not ever!"

"I'm sorry, boss," his longtime spotter said, as his butt pushed away from Mick, his hands lifted up to shield him from further harm, the barbells falling away from him. The pain that was ripping through his body was visible all over his face. "I apologize, sir. I didn't mean any harm. I didn't mean any disrespect. Please forgive me, sir. Please forgive me!"

But as quickly as Mick had knocked him

down, he wasn't thinking about him anymore. He was thinking about his niece, and Boston, and why in the world were the Feds fucking with them like this?

Charles was leaned against his Jaguar, with his arms folded and his legs crossed at the ankle. His shades shielded his worried eyes as he watched the Gulfstream Jet descend from the clouds and land at the Boston airstrip. Charles was a wealthy man. By Jericho's standards, he was the wealthiest. But his kid brother Mick, like their cousins the Gabrinis, was among the mega-rich. And like the superrich, Mick's excesses often astounded Charles, even as the mobster in Mick concerned him. But in times like these, he was glad to have Mick in his corner. They were up against the FBI, and they were the point. Mick, in Charles's mind, was the counterpoint.

The steps of the plane dropped down and within seconds Mick descended in his flapping black suitcoat. He hurried down and across the tarmac alone. Men like him usually ran with entourages, especially at a time like this. But there was no one waiting but Charles as if Mick didn't trust anybody else to handle this situation but himself, and his big brother.

"Where's Jenay?" Mick asked as he

approached.

"I wouldn't let her come. She's still recovering."

Mick stared at Charles. "Recovering from what?"

Charles didn't keep his brother in the loop. He regretted it. "Somebody shot up the B & B a couple weeks ago. One of the bullets grazed her arm."

"Any idea who might have fired the shots?"

"I saw the prick," Charles said. "Some political agitator named Abe Norris, although we found out that's not his real name. But that's all we found out about him. He was protesting my ownership rights in Jericho. I'm a monopoly, let him and his ilk tell it."

"He's still at large?"

Charles nodded. "He's still out there, yeah."

Mick stared at his brother. "You didn't think I needed to know this?"

"I had some men working it. I thought I had it under control. I didn't know this shit was going to turn the way it turned. I thought that would be enough."

"It is never enough," Mick said, "when it comes to our enemies. It always turns. And we have to face facts."

"Such as?"

"Because of my involvement in this matter, perhaps my enemies have become yours."

Charles lifted his shades above his head, as if he had to get a better view of his brother. He knew the gravity of what he spoke. "You think that's possible? You think somebody's using what happened with Carly to get to you?"

"I am not verse enough in what is going on to reach the ultimate conclusion right now," Mick admitted. "But yes, that is what I think."

Charles closed his eyes and shook his head. "Good Lord," he said. Then he looked at Mick. "But how could they have found out? Nobody knew but us." Then Charles added: "And your men."

"I understand your concern. My men are not fools. They know what will befall them if they cross me. But, I am not foolish either. Every one of the men who worked for me that night are being round up as we speak. If it was one of them, I will know."

Charles nodded. He respected Mick's efficiency.

"What about Carly?" Mick asked. "What is her status?"

"They have her here in Boston. In jail. Brent and Makayla are heading over there right now to try to win her release. Or at least see her and make sure she's okay."

"And who is protecting Jenay?"

Charles loved the fact that Mick cared deeply for Jenay. If Charles was his father-figure, Jenay was his mother-figure, and he seemed to place them both above the rest. "Tony's protecting her and Bonita. I ordered him to make certain they both stay at home until I get back." Charles frowned. "It was supposed to be Jenay's first day back at work. But it can't be helped."

"No, it can't," Mick said. "But don't worry. It is probably not her they are after."

"But we can never be too sure until we are," Charles said.

Mick nodded. "Right," he said.

And then they got into Charles's Jaguar, and Charles sped away.

It took several trips around the various blocks until the two men were convinced they were not being followed. And then they drove to the spot on the preserve just outside of Boston where they oversaw the burial of Ethan Campbell's body. But it wasn't even close. They didn't have to get out of the car. For the marker they laid to identify the body, a stone of a unique shape, had been rolled away and the ground upturned in dramatic fashion. The body had not only been dug up and removed, but the grave diggers didn't care who knew. The *in your face* nature of the dig suggested to Mick and Charles immediately that whoever dug up that grave wanted them to know. They wanted to be certain that the allegations the FBI leveled against Carly were substantiated. The Feds had the body. And somebody put that body in Carly's old house.

"We're in trouble, Mick," Charles said as the reality of what they were witnessing began to sink in.

CHAPTER SIXTEEN

Trevor Reese entered the Boston police station within minutes of Carly's arrival. He removed his gloves as he hurried to the information desk. "Where is she?" he asked urgently.

"Where is who, sir?" the desk sergeant responded.

"Where is the young black woman that just arrived here?"

"The one with the Feds?" he asked.

"Yes, I imagine so." Trevor wasn't sure if the FBI would have escorted her here, but he knew it was plausible. "Where is she?"

"They just took her in the back, sir. To process her in. Then they're going to question her."

That seemed backwards to Trevor as he hurried to the security door. "Open it," he ordered. "And tell the chief I want to see him."

"Yes, sir," the desk sergeant said as he pressed the button, the door unlocked, and Trevor hurried inside.

A patrolman walked over to the sergeant. "Still throwing his weight around," he said.

"You should have told him to go fuck himself."

"And lose my ability to feed my family?" the sergeant responded. "Not to mention I just might lose my life when that asshole gets through with me? You go tell him."

The patrolman looked as if he just might, but then he walked away.

"Yeah, I thought so," the sergeant said as he picked up the phone to notify the chief.

Behind the security door, Trevor made his way toward Booking. When he saw Carly standing there, waiting next in line to be booked, his heart dropped. He wanted to hurry to her, the way he hurried to Boston when he got the word. But he composed himself. He'd do what he could to get her out of this jeopardy, and then get out of her life again. He erred by going to her house in the first place. That was a disaster. He almost showed his hand too much. He wasn't going to make that same mistake again.

He walked over to Carly just as she walked up to the window and lifted her hand for the fingerprint man.

He took her hand in his. "Not yet," he said.

Carly was astounded to see Trevor in that police station. Didn't he say he was on his way to Canada? How did he get back to Boston?

And why was he here, in this police station? She was as puzzled as she was confused.

"You wanted to see me, Mr. Reese?" a voice said behind them.

They both turned. It was the chief of the Boston police department.

"Yes," Trevor said. "We need to talk."

"Is this young lady the subject?"

"Yes," said Trevor.

"The FBI are waiting to have a round or two with her."

"I understand."

"There's just so much I can do."

"I understand," Trevor said again. "We need to talk."

The chief didn't like it, Carly could tell he didn't like it one bit. But to her own astonishment, he caved. And escorted them out of the Booking room, and down the hall to his own office.

Brent and Makayla entered the police department certain that the most they could hope for was a meeting with Carly. But when they weren't getting even that much from the desk sergeant, they decided to change their approach.

"I'm her attorney," Makayla said, "and I demand to see my client."

Makayla was an attorney, but as the district attorney for Jericho County she wasn't anybody's private attorney. But tough times called for tough measures and she didn't hesitate. She knew Brent, and she knew her in-laws. They were not going to rest until somebody eyeballed Carly in that jailhouse.

"Her attorney?" the desk sergeant asked.

"Yes, sir. And I demand to see my client."

"What are you doing here with the chief of police if you're her attorney?" the officer asked. Then he looked at Brent. "Didn't you say you was the police chief up in Maine?"

"I am, but I also said I was Carly Sinatra's brother. I'm here in that capacity."

"With her lawyer?"

"That's right," Brent said. He and Makayla were not the kind of people who lied easily, and this was uncomfortable as hell for both of them. But he'd do much more, and did already, for Carly.

"You can't go in," the sergeant said. "They aren't letting her see any relatives just yet. But I might be able to give her lawyer a few minutes."

"Fine," Brent said. It wasn't, but it was better than not seeing her at all.

"Have a seat and I'll look into it," the sergeant said.

Brent had a feeling that it was a stall tactic, but he didn't argue with the man. Not yet anyway. He and Makayla took a seat. He crossed his legs, placed his big hat on his knee, and placed her hand in his.

It would take several minutes, but the side door eventually opened and a tall, well-dressed white man walked out. Brent and Makayla both looked at him. "Good afternoon," he said. "Are you here for Carly?"

Brent and Makayla stood up. "Yes," Brent said.

"She's right behind me," the gentleman said. "She's just been released."

Makayla looked at Brent. Was this a joke? "Released?" Brent asked the man.

"Why, yes."

"And you know this how?"

The side door opened again, and Carly walked out. "Carly!" Makayla said and ran to her. They hugged.

But Brent was still looking at this stranger. "Who are you?" he asked.

"Trevor Reese," the gentleman said, extending his hand. "Carly's former employer."

Brent thought something smelled fishy. Now he knew it. This guy showed up at his father's house out of the blue, and then shortly thereafter Carly was arrested. And now he managed to get her released? Brent looked at Carly and Makayla. "Wait here," he ordered.

But Carly was confused. "They let me go, Brent. Why should I have to wait in this place?"

"Because I said so," Brent said, and walked out of the exit doors.

Makayla held Carly closer. "It'll be okay," she said. "He just wants to make sure."

Carly looked at Trevor. He smiled and hunched his shoulder. "Anyway," he said, "I've got a plane to catch. I leave you in the hands of your family." Then his look changed. It was almost an affectionate look, if Carly had to describe it. But she knew better. Trevor Reese never showed affection to anyone. "Take care," he said to her, nodded at Makayla, and left.

Makayla looked at Carly. "Were you two guys an item when you lived in Boston?"

"No," Carly said, still reeling from her arrest, from that night in Boston two-and-a-half months ago, and from Trevor reemergence in her life. "It was a complete employer-employee relationship. Totally professional."

"But he's the one who showed up at your parents' home this morning. Isn't he?"

Carly nodded. "Yes," she said. "Out of the blue he showed up. Then he said he was on his way to Canada. But then he's here within minutes of my arrival. He wouldn't even let them process me in, or place me in a jail cell."

Makayla was surprised. "He has that kind of pull?"

Carly nodded. "Apparently so because they wouldn't do it. Then he started calling in all kinds of favors and the next thing I knew, the commissioner showed up and said I was free to go. There was no evidence to support that I had anything to do with Ethan Campbell's death."

"No evidence?" Makayla asked. "Even though they found his body in the house you used to rent?"

"Right," Carly said, and looked at Makayla. "Weird, hun?"

Makayla nodded. "I'd say," she said.

Charles and Mick were driving back to the airstrip. Mick was in deep thought while Charles drove. Silence reigned supreme, as talking about what they saw at that burial site would only produce speculation on top of speculation and none of it would give them any more information. Until the car phone rang. When Charles saw that it was Brent's cell phone calling, he quickly pressed the speaker button of his car phone. "Brent, hey."

"Found anything?" Brent asked.

"Yeah," Charles responded. "An empty grave."

Brent closed his eyes. "Don't tell me that. Geez."

"How's Carly?"

Brent opened his eyes. The news of the empty grave was only part of the story. "That's why I'm calling. They released her, Dad."

Charles almost slammed on brakes. Mick was stunned too. "They released her?" Charles asked. "They had the hearing already?"

"No. No hearing."

Charles frowned. "Then what are you talking about, Brent? They released her on her own recognizance?"

"They released her," Brent said. "They never booked her. They will not be filing charges."

Charles ran his hand through his thick hair. It should have been great news, but he and Mick knew it wasn't. After seeing that burial site, they knew it couldn't be.

"And Dad," Brent added, "guess who was behind her release?"

"Who?" Mick quickly asked.

"Trevor Reese," Brent said.

Charles couldn't believe it. "Trevor Reese? But he said he was on his way to Canada. How the hell did he get to Boston?"

"Who is he?" Mick asked.

"Carly's former boss," Charles responded. "The guy who represented Ethan Campbell."

Even Mick's heart began to hammer. "Where is he now?" he asked.

"He just left the station," Brent said. "I don't know where he's headed."

Mick pulled out his cell phone.

"What do you want me to do, Dad?" Brent asked.

Charles looked at Mick. "You thinking what I'm thinking?"

Mick nodded. "Hell yeah."

"Get Carly and Makayla," Charles ordered his son, "and get your asses to the airstrip."

"The airstrip?" Brent asked.

"Get to my plane," Mick said as he searched his phone for a particular number. "We need everybody together until we can figure this shit out."

Brent didn't even question it, or what they were going to do about the cars they drove to Boston. His father had called in his Uncle Mick. His father had called in that level of backup. It was out of his hands now.

CHAPTER SEVENTEEN

While the entire Sinatra clan were gathered in the family room, Charles, Mick, and Brent were gathered together in the study. Charles was seated behind the desk, Mick was seated on the edge of the desk beside Charles, and Brent was leaned against the window behind the desk watching and listening to them both.

"I don't know how it can't be one of your men, Mick," Charles was saying. "Who the hell else would know?"

"It is not one of my men. They have been checked and double-checked. They check out."

"But who else but some mobster would do such a thing?" Charles asked, his face flustered. "Move a fucking body? And take it back to Carly's old house? Whoever did this knows what happened in that house."

Mick knew what Charles spoke was the truth. "They're coming here," he said.

"Who?" Brent asked.

Mick exhaled. "My men. The ones from that night in Boston. They're on their way to Jericho."

Brent unfolded his arms and looked at his father. Charles was staring at Mick. "You suspect something?" Charles asked. "I thought you said they checked out."

"They did. But that's the problem. You pose the question yourself. Who the hell else would know?"

"Maybe somebody followed you guys to that burial site," Brent said.

"Nobody followed us," Mick said.

"But what if they did?"

"They did not!" Mick blared and slammed his fist on the desk. "I've been burying bodies my entire adult life, boy! All my life! Not one of those bodies has ever been discovered. Not one!"

"Until now," Charles said firmly, looking Mick dead in the eye. Mick looked at him. "And you get control of that temper around my son," Charles added.

Mick let out a harsh exhale. No man would have ever had the nerve to tell Mick to get control of anything and expect to live to tell about it. Except his big brother Charles. A man he respected above any man alive. The man who raised him, after their father went to prison for murdering their mother, with love and an iron fist. He settled back down.

Brent continued to stare at his uncle. He

knew who he was. He knew he was Mick the Tick. As in an explosive ticking time bomb of a temper. As in mob boss who handled all kinds of horrific mob matters. He knew his uncle was responsible for some seriously fucked-up deeds in his life. And now Brent and his father and mother, not to mention Carly, were caught up in that life too. But Brent knew this deed wasn't his uncle's fault. They were the ones who called him in.

The door to the study opened, and Jenay walked in. Charles looked at her. He hated that she had to be involved in any of this. "Hey, babe," he said.

"I heard loud voices," she said as she walked toward the desk. "Everything alright?"

Mick stood and began to pace the floor. Brent shook his head and turned toward the window, looking out onto the well maintained grounds of his parents' home. Charles leaned forward. "We're going in circles," he said.

"So now you're a circular firing squad?" Jenay asked.

Charles managed to smile. Jenay always had a way with words. "Something like that," he said. "Where's everybody?"

"In the family room."

"Carly okay?"

Jenay nodded. "Donnie and Ash are asking

her a lot of questions, but she's weathering the storm. She's pleased to be out, that's for sure. But she's worried, Charles." Then Jenay frowned. "As am I."

Charles hurried up from his desk, walked around, and pulled Jenay into his arms. Mick and Brent watched as Charles held her tightly. "It's going to be alright," he said to her. "It's going to be alright, Jean."

Brent was particularly concerned. He knew, whenever his father used Jenay's rarely used nickname, it meant he was taking it to heart. He might not have been saying just the opposite, but he apparently wasn't at all sure if everything was going to be alright.

Charles leaned slightly back and lifted Jenay's chin. "You know we're going to get through this," he said. "Right?"

Jenay was still anguished. She was not the kind of woman who could pretend otherwise. "But who moved that body, Charlie?" she asked. "And what else do they know? Do they know that Carly . . ." She couldn't bring herself to finish the sentence. Charles pulled her back into his big arms.

When they heard a knock on the study door, all of them looked in that direction. "Yes?" Charles asked.

The door was opened, and Tony stepped

inside. "Sorry to disturb you guys," he said, "but a Ross Falcone is here to see Uncle Mick."

Charles looked at Mick. Mick nodded. Charles looked back at his son. "Send him in," he said.

Tony glanced at Jenay's worried face, and Brent's, and felt a twinge of hurt that he was not included in what was obviously a family crisis. But he was a patient man. His dad would let him know when the time was right. He left the study.

"Who is this Falcone guy, Unc?" Brent asked.

"One of my men," Mick said.

"He was there that night?"

Mick began walking toward the desk. "No. He wasn't a part of that crew. He's been looking into our Trevor Reese problem for me."

"Good," Charles said. "I hope he has some intel."

Mick sat on the edge of the desk as the door re-opened, and a tall, muscular man in a business suit walked in. "Hey, boss," he said when he saw Mick's familiar face. He remembered Charles's face that night too, but dared not say so. Men in his line of work never told.

"What did you find out, Fal?" Mick asked.

Falcone walked up to the desk and handed

Mick a folder. Mick immediately handed the folder to Charles. "Tell me," he said to Falcone as Charles began reviewing the folder.

"Trevor Reese runs a highly successful marketing firm. Reese Marketing. It's out of Boston."

"Where Carly worked?" Mick asked Charles and Jenay.

"That's where she worked," Jenay responded, "yes."

"It's successful as hell, boss," Falcone said, "with a powerful client list."

"I see," Charles said, reviewing the file.

"But it's a front," Falcone said.

Brent unfolded his arms and began to move toward the others. Even Charles stopped reviewing the paperwork and looked too. "A front?" he asked.

"It's a front," Falcone repeated while nodding his head.

Mick was surprised too. "A front for what?"

"That's the thing, boss. We have no idea. We couldn't find out shit about this guy."

"Then how do you know his marketing firm is a front?" Brent asked.

"That doesn't mean it's not legit, Brent," Mick explained. "I run Sinatra Industries. An international corporation. That's legit too. But sometimes legitimate organizations can help to mask other things."

"You mean like illegitimate business interests?" Brent asked.

"Like that, yes," Mick said.

Charles's heart began to pound. "Are you telling us," he asked Falcone, "that Trevor Reese is a mobster?"

"I can't say that he is," Falcone responded. "I can't say that he isn't. We just don't know. The only reason we know that marketing firm of his is a front for other things is because of his activities and his schedules over the years. This guy is all over the place. But he has no clients in those places. None. Like right now. He flew on his private jet to Canada. But we checked his client logs. He has no clients in Canada."

"But he could have a new client he's going to meet," Jenay said. "I don't see where that's determinative of anything."

"And I agree with you, ma'am," Falcone said, "if that was all we had. But check this out, boss," he added, turning back to Mick. "When he got there, he didn't go to some office or some house to meet with somebody."

"Where did he go?" Mick asked.

"He went to a warehouse for the meeting."

Mick knew what that meant. He had more

than his share of meetings in warehouses too, and none of those meetings were legit. "Was he under heavy security?" he asked Falcone.

"The heaviest," Falcone responded. "Our men couldn't get close enough to see who he was meeting with or anything like that."

"But you're certain something was undercover?" Brent asked.

"Warehouse meetings are never legit," Mick pointed out. "That shit has mob written all over it."

"Or Fed," Charles said.

Everybody looked at him. "Fed?" Brent asked.

"Maybe that's why he knew so quickly about Carly's incarceration. Maybe he has inside information. How else would he have known?"

"That's true," Jenay said. "But maybe he was the one who led the FBI to Carly in the first place. They knocked on our front door in less than a half hour after he left."

"But why would he get her released with no charges filed," Brent asked, "if he led them to her?"

"So he could play the hero," Charles responded to his son, "and Carly would confide in him."

"And he would try to get her to confess to

what happened that night," Jenay added.

Falcone looked at Mick. "It makes sense, boss," he said.

Mick was beginning to warm to their reasoning too. "Yeah, it does. It's possible," he said.

"But how can we find out?" Brent asked. "How can we test this possibility?"

"Only one way," Mick responded. Then he looked at Charles. "Carly is going to have to bait him out," he said.

But Charles was already shaking his head. "No way."

"It's the only way, Charles," Mick said. "If I was certain he was mob, then her services would not be needed. I would know how to bait him myself. But if he's Fed as you suggest, then we can't do anything until we find out what level of Fed are we dealing with. Until we find out just what is he up to concerning Carly's situation."

"And how is my daughter expected to get to the bottom of this?" Charles asked.

"This is her life. This is her future we're talking about. She'll wine him, she'll dine him, she'll give him whatever he wants. She'll fuck him if she has to."

"Now just a minute!" Brent started, but Charles held up his hand.

"Go on," Charles said to Mick.

"It's the only way we can find out what this guy is up to. If my men couldn't find out shit, that means it's deep."

"And dangerous?" Charles asked his brother.

Mick couldn't lie to him. "Always that," he said. Then he exhaled. "Look, I know she's your sweet little girl and you love her dearly. But she wasn't so sweet and little when she stabbed that man damn near thirty times. She was all grown up then. She's got to work for her freedom. She's got to fight for her life. That's what will be expected of her."

Mick's cell phone began ringing as Jenay and Brent looked at Charles. They hated that it had come to this, but they knew Mick was right. Charles knew it too. That was the hardest part for him.

"What are you thinking, Charles?" Jenay asked him as Mick walked away to answer his phone call.

"I'm thinking Carly's been through hell already. I'm thinking I don't want to take her through anymore. But," he added with a sense of resignation in his voice, "there doesn't appear to be any other way. Unfortunately," he said, looking at Jenay, "Mick is right. It's her life, and her freedom we're talking about."

Mick ended his call and looked at Charles. "My men are in town."

"Then let's go," Charles said, getting ready to leave.

Brent was about to follow the two men, but Charles put his hand on Brent's chest and stopped him. Brent looked at his father. "What?" he asked.

"You aren't going anywhere."

"Dad!"

"You have a town to run, and a family to oversee. *My* family. You stay here. We'll be back."

Brent was accustomed to being on the front line of the action, not the backseat player. But it was his father and Mick Sinatra. He understood. He didn't like it, but he understood. He nodded. "Yes, sir," he said.

Charles gave Brent a double pat on his chest. Brent was the best oldest son a man could ever hope to have. He felt blessed to have him. Charles kissed Jenay, pulled her in his arms again, and then he and Mick left.

Brent looked at Jenay. "Are they serious?" he asked. "Is Daddy really going to let Carly anywhere near some guy who just might be Mafia just because Uncle Mick wants him to? How can he rely on that?"

Jenay, still holding the folder on Trevor

Reese, saw the anguish in Brent's eyes. She pulled him into her arms. Brent's eyes squeezed shut. This was getting to him, and Jenay knew it. "Trust your father," she whispered in his ear as she held his big body. "He loves all of us, but he sees a vulnerability in Carly that draws her to him." Then she pulled back and looked Brent in his beautiful green eyes. "Daddy will never let anything happen to her. Rely on that."

Brent looked at her and nodded. He always understood why his father loved Jenay above all those other women he used to have, but he understood it right now more than ever. And he hugged her again.

They sat in a cargo van on the outskirts of Jericho. Three men sitting strong, all lined up against the white metal wall. The fourth man, Craw, was standing, and when a knock was heard on the door, he was the one to slide it open. Mick and Charles got in and sat in seats across from the men.

"Why are we here, boss?" one of them asked.

"We had a breach," Mick said. "I have a grave robber on my payroll."

The men looked at each other. "A grave robber, boss?" one asked. "What do you mean?"

"The Boston job. What happened?"

"Nothing happened. We did our work and got out. Like we always do. We didn't rob that grave. We didn't say a word about that job. We've been working for you for years. We wouldn't do anything like that!"

Then it suddenly dawned on Mick. He frowned. And looked at Craw. "Where the fuck is Anzino?" he asked.

Craw shook his head. "We couldn't locate him."

This surprised even Charles.

Mick frowned. "What do you mean you couldn't locate him?"

"I couldn't locate him. He didn't return my calls. It happens. He's probably on vacation or something."

Mick stared at Craw as if he had just insulted him. Before Charles knew what was happening, Mick jumped up, grabbed Craw and slammed his head against the van's metal wall. He continued to slam the man's head, drawing blood, and Charles wanted to stop him. But these men were Mick's men, and none of them were saints. Mick knew what he was doing.

"You tell me that one of my men won't respond to an urgent callout," Mick said, "and you don't think that kind of information isn't an important piece of information? What the fuck do you think a callout means? What the fuck were you thinking?"

"I wasn't thinking like that, boss," Craw said nervously. "Mag was just the driver. I didn't think his not answering was a big deal."

Wrong answer, the other men thought as Mick, angered by the response, banged Craw's head even harder. *"No big deal*?" Mick screamed. "You think I'm doing this for my fucking health? Now he knows we had a callout. Now he knows his ass is on the grill! You stupid fuck! And it's all because you unilaterally decided that my decision to find out if I had a breach didn't need to include one of the men who could have caused the breach!"

"I didn't mean it like that, boss. I thought you just wanted to talk to the grave diggers. Anzino was the driver. He's never been deep in the action."

"Until now, motherfucker," Mick said, and angrily released Craw. "Until now!"

Craw, bleeding from the ear, slid down to the floor in excruciating pain. Charles expected the other men to help him, but they didn't move a muscle. They, instead, took their cues from Mick. And Mick just stood there.

Charles watched his brother stand there as

if he was catching his breath. Most men in that position would regret losing their temper that way. But Charles didn't see regret anywhere on Mick's handsome face. He saw anger and frustration, maybe even a little rage. But he never saw regret.

Mick looked at his men. "Remain in this area. Check into a motel."

"Yes, sir," the remaining men said.

"Stay put until you hear from me." Then he looked at Craw. "And that includes you too, asshole."

"Yes, yes, sir," Craw said, the pain causing him to sweat profusely. He wiped the sweat from his brow. "Yes, yes, sir!"

Mick walked over to the door of the van, slid it open, and stepped out. Charles looked at Craw, and then stepped out too.

Mick had a handkerchief out, and was wiping his hands.

"You're going after him?" Charles asked.

Mick looked at Charles as if he had lost his mind. "Does a lion roar?" he asked.

Charles nodded. He knew it was an obvious question when he asked it. But he needed to know Mick's thinking. "You believe your man Anzino may be the breach?"

"He may. I will find out, believe that. It will probably take some time, so don't expect overnight results. It could take weeks. If he's guilty of betraying me, he'll be hiding deep down undercover. But I'll work that end until he's found. Count on that."

Then Mick looked hard at Charles. "But Carly will need to work Trevor Reese. She's got to find out what he knows, and what he's up to. Anzino might have told about the grave, and might have even unearthed that body. But there's no way he took it back to Carly's house by himself. He had power behind him."

Charles stared at Mick. "Trevor Reese's kind of power?"

Mick nodded. "That kind, yes. And I know you hate the thought of it, but it's up to your daughter. Carly has got to be the one to crack his ironclad code. My men haven't been able to do it. We can't do it the traditional way. She has to be the one."

CHAPTER EIGHTEEN

Trevor Reese glanced at his watch one more time as he sat in the restaurant at the Jericho Inn. Carly had actually phoned his office and left a message for him to get in contact with her. He was still in Canada at the time, but he eventually returned her call. On his way back to Boston, Carly had said, she wondered if he could meet with her.

It was exactly what he had hoped to hear, and he quickly agreed. Now she was late. He did not like tardiness.

"Hello, Mr. Reese."

He looked up and saw the lady he remembered being introduced to him as Carly's mother standing beside his table. He rose to his feet. "Mrs. Sinatra, hello."

Jenay smiled. "Welcome to the Jericho Inn."

"Thank you." He did his due diligence after he met her and discovered that her husband owned this place, so he wasn't entirely surprised to see her there. But she didn't know that. "You're here for dinner too?"

"Hardly," Jenay said with a faint smile. "I

215

run this place. I hope the service so far has been good."

"It's been excellent. Thank you."

"You're waiting for my daughter. Correct?"

She wasn't being coy about it, and he liked her directness. "That's correct," he said. "She's late."

"She's usually very punctual, so I suspect she'll show up momentarily. If you would like I can phone and see what's keeping her?"

"That won't be necessary. But thank you."

Jenay gave him a smile, and headed over to the bar. Tony was seated at the bar with a bullseye view of Trevor Reese. Jenay sat beside him. "He's a very charming man," she said.

"So was Hitler," Tony responded. "Where's Carly? She should have been here by now."

"She'll be here. Daddy thought it would be a good idea to see how long he would be willing to wait for her."

"Why would that matter?" Tony asked.

"If he patiently waits, then that usually means he genuinely came because he cares about her, or at least have genuine feelings for her."

"And if he impatiently waits?" Tony asked.

"Then, as Ashley would put it, *he ain't about nothing good*."

Tony smiled. "Your verdict?" he asked.

"He must have checked his watch ten times since he's been sitting there."

"He ain't about nothing good?" Tony asked.

"Bingo," Jenay said. Then a worried look appeared on her face. "Unfortunately," she added, as she stood up. "Just may sure you keep your eyes on her. I know Uncle Mick has his people around this place, although I haven't spotted any of them."

"You aren't supposed to spot them," Tony said. "If you do, then they aren't doing a good job. But you know Daddy. He made me come as backup. He isn't going to let his daughter meet with a man, especially a man they have determined is dangerous, without covering her like a blanket."

Jenay smiled. "Thank God for Daddy. He looks out for us well."

"Speak for yourself," Tony said. "Nobody's looking out for me."

Jenay laughed and looked toward the entrance. Carly was just arriving. She patted Tony on the shoulder. "Alright, hot shot, your sister is here. Do the job your father ordered you to do."

"Will do," Tony said as he sipped his drink. Jenay headed back across the room, to the front desk inside the lobby of the B & B.

Trevor looked at Carly as she entered the Inn. There was no denying her beauty, he thought as she headed his way. But it was a tortured beauty to him. When she first started working for him, he used to observe her daily. And something struck with him. She presented as a strong, confident woman, but what he saw instead was a quiet desperation in Carly, like a caged bird in an open cage. Every time other birds flew past her, he could tell she wanted to fly away too. But she, instead, as if to prove just how good a bird she truly was, stayed in her cage. And she waited. What he couldn't figure out then, and still couldn't figure out now, was what in the world was she waiting on?

She wore a sleeveless bubble dress that highlighted her narrow waist and shapely legs, with matching heels and purse. With her long hair dropped down her back in waves, and her big eyes soft but sharp as a sword, and her flawless brown skin, she was a sight to behold. He wanted to fuck her so bad he could feel his penis throb. And he was going to fuck the shit out of her, among other things. But in time. He rose to his feet as she arrived at his table.

"Sorry I'm late," she said cheerfully.

"Quite alright," he said with a smile of his own. "I don't care for tardiness, but I will let you slide this time."

Carly smiled as he moved over and pulled her chair out for her. "Thank you," she said, AND sat down. Her heart was pounding, and she was as nervous as she'd ever been, but she was a master at wearing the mask. She laid it on thick tonight.

Trevor sat across from her and watched her as the waitress arrived and took her drink and food orders.

"They know me here," Carly said, "so we'll get good service."

"Your father owns the place," Trevor said. "Or is that wrong information?"

She had hoped he didn't know that. Because the more he knew, the more research into her family life he would have had to do. Which would only confirm what her father and uncle were saying all along: he was up to something, and it more than likely wasn't something good. "No," she said. "Your information is correct."

"I also discovered that this town does not like him very well. But of course they have no reason to dislike him, right?"

"Wrong," Carly said. "They have plenty of reasons. A lot of them have business with him, or rent from him, and he doesn't go along with their nonsense. He holds them accountable for paying their rent on time or for fulfilling their obligations under any contracts they may have with him. If they fail to perform, he cuts them off. He shows no mercy. They have plenty of reasons to think of him as nothing short of an asshole. Are their reasons fair? No. Are their reasons justifiable? Yes."

Trevor smiled. "That is why I have always liked you, Carly," he admitted. "That is why I hired you in the first place. You do not bullshit. You tell it like it is."

When he said that, Carly outwardly smiled. But inwardly she felt horrible. She always liked her former boss too. She liked his professionalism. She liked his no nonsense approach to every problem. She liked the fact that he was this great looking guy who didn't fool around with anyone at work nor allow his employees to so much as glimpse his personal life in any way, shape, or form. He was still the only man she had ever worked with who didn't try to get her in his bed. And that was despite the fact that he was the only man she ever worked with whom she would have loved to get in bed with. But he never crossed that line. She respected Trevor Reese.

And all of this talk about him having something to do with digging up Ethan Campbell's grave, despite her knowledge of him, was making her feel uneasy. She worked with this man for months. He had a national reputation for his integrity and ethical standards. She couldn't imagine him being involved with such hideousness.

The waitress returned with her drink order, and refreshed Trevor's drink. When the waitress left their table, Trevor looked at Carly. "I'm pleased you phoned me," he said. "I thought you were a little upset that I had visited you at your home."

Carly wasn't going to lie. She was very upset that morning. But she knew how to pivot. You knew how to stay focused on why she was there to begin with. "You're the man who was able to get me out of that Boston jail. You're the man who miraculously got them to drop the charges. I'll always be grateful to you for that."

"Ah, that was nothing," Trevor said with a wave of the hand. "You're worth every effort I demonstrate."

Carly stared at him. "But weren't you a little curious about Ethan's body? They said they found it in the house I used to rent. I didn't put it there, I was in Jericho living my life, but somebody did."

"I was curious, yes," Trevor said. "But I did my research. Your father has many enemies, and not just the local ones here in Jericho. I concluded that somebody tried to get to him through you. Besides, I know you. There is no way in hell that you would have been foolish enough to leave a dead body in your house."

"But they weren't just claiming that I left his body there," Carly said. "They were claiming that I killed him and left his body there."

"Yes, I know," Trevor said.

Carly stared at Trevor. "But doesn't that part disturb you? The fact that the authorities arrested me for the *murder* of Ethan Campbell?"

Trevor seemed to think about that question. Then he looked at her. "Ethan was an asshole. Which is fine. He has that right. But he was rapist too, and we both knew it. He raped that child and probably would have raped others too. Whoever killed him did the world a favor, in my book. Whoever killed him probably had no choice. So no, Carly, that part of the equation doesn't disturb me at all."

He and Carly shared a long stare. She didn't want to go there, but she knew she had to go there. The FBI could have him wired, her uncle Mick had already warned her, so she knew her words had to be carefully chosen. "Do you think I killed Ethan Campbell?" she asked him point blank. If he was an FBI operative or informant, he would take the ball and run with it. If he wasn't the Fed, he would punt.

"I don't know," Trevor responded, "and I don't care. I have enough business of my own, and that is not my business. You needn't declare your innocence to me, or confess your sins to me. I don't give a shit, to be honest. Not when it concerns a bastard like Ethan Campbell. I'm just glad you're out of their custody. I'm just glad I got there before they could formally book you in."

"You wouldn't have been able to get me out if they had?" Carly asked.

Trevor smiled. "I didn't say that," he said. "It would have made my job more difficult, yes. But for you? I would have pulled it off."

Carly smiled too. He was a charmer alright, she thought. No doubt about that. But she couldn't be fooled by it either. Her father and uncle didn't have him on their shit list for the hell of it. They didn't have her calling him up and asking to meet with him, when there could be danger involved, for their health. Despite all she knew about him, and believed him to be, he might be attempting to bring her down. She had to fight to stay up. This meeting, they told her, was the beginning of her battle. "How was your trip to Canada?" she asked him, careful to stick to the script.

"It was okay," Trevor responded.

That was the Trevor that Carly remembered. Every time anybody at work would ask him something about his life, he would blow it off. *It was okay. It's alright. It's fine.* Never anything more than that. But unlike when she worked for him, it was her job tonight to sift him out. It was her job to get personal with him. "Did you get the result you were looking for?" she asked.

"Perhaps," Trevor responded.

Carly smiled. "In other words, mind my own business. Right?"

Trevor smiled. "What about you?" he asked.

Carly was impressed with how smoothly he changed the subject. "Me?" she asked.

"Still enjoying your teaching job?"

"Oh. Why, yes. I'm enjoying it."

"It's a far cry from the job you did for me in Boston."

"Yes, it is."

"I was hoping that was what this meeting was about."

Carly gave him a puzzled look. "Excuse me?"

"I was hoping you wanted to meet with me

so that you could ask to come back to work for me."

Carly's heart began to swell. He came, not because he wanted to feel her out and get her to confess to Ethan's killing. He came because he wanted her back. She suspected he didn't know a thing about that night in Boston! At least that was her hope. But she knew she had to tread cautiously. She could just be blinded by her affection for him. "I see," she said.

"I always go hard for talent," Trevor said. "You know that. Talent is the name of the game for me. You have it in bucket loads, Carly," he added.

Carly smiled. "Thank you, Mr. Reese."

"Mr. Reese? While having drinks together? It's Trevor to you, missy."

Carly laughed. And she suddenly realized that he was the only person, since her world tilted that night in Boston, who had been able to make her laugh. "Trevor," she said.

"So am I correct to assume that is why you phoned?" he asked. "To get back into my good graces?"

"Well yes and no," Carly responded, careful not to tell an outright lie. "I've been thinking about going back to Boston and resuming my career, yes, I have. But I don't know if I want to leave my family just yet."

"The emergency that caused you to quit your job in the first place is still problematic?" Trevor asked.

Carly wondered if he knew something. "Excuse me?"

"The reason you cited for leaving my firm. You mentioned a family emergency. Is that still the reason that keeps you here?"

"Oh! No. That's been resolved. But I'm back in the habit of being with my family every day. It's a tough habit to break."

"Then you must look on the bright side," Trevor said. "Is it better that you eyeball your family every day, or get back on track with your real career? A career, by the by, that was taking you straight to the top."

Carly knew it too. But she had to push the envelope. Her father told her so. If he was up to something, it would be revealed. "You ever wondered about why I left it all behind like that?" She stared at him after she asked it. If he knew what happened to Ethan that night and her role in Ethan's death, and he wanted a confession as her father and uncle believed, despite what he had just told her, then she'd just given him the opening he needed to try it. She'd just given him the hammer to hammer her with.

But Trevor punted again. "I didn't have to

wonder," he said. "Your family comes first. Someone in your family needed you, so you forgot about yourself and aided them. It is an admirable quality. One I wish I had."

There was a pause, and Carly could see a look that could have passed for regret in his eyes.

"So no," he added, "I never wonder why you left your career behind. With your talent, it's just a matter of picking it back up someday." Then he smiled. "I was hoping today would be that day. But I can wait." He stared into Carly's eyes. "You're worth it."

"So that we're clear," Carly said. "If I decide to return to Boston, you'll take me back?"

Trevor stared at her. He thought he'd already made that clear. "In a heartbeat," he said, to be clearer.

Carly smiled and sipped her drink. He didn't know a thing. He wasn't trying to pick her brain. It was early still, but at least for right now she could not have been more pleased.

The SUV pulled up four doors down from the small block house. Charles was seated in the front seat, and Mick was in the back. Mick checked his gun, to make sure it was fully loaded, and then placed it in the back of his pants along the small of his back. "There's a 7-Eleven around the block," he said to his driver. "Wait for us there."

"Yes, sir," the driver responded as Mick and Charles got out of the vehicle, walked onto the sidewalk of the suburban neighborhood, and made their way to the house. They were back in Boston, after a quick ride on Mick's plane, after word came that Anzino had been spotted. They couldn't get to Boston fast enough.

But now they were walking leisurely, as if they were two businessmen on a neighborhood stroll, or Jehovah's Witnesses ready to hand out literature. They didn't exactly fit in, but they didn't stand out either.

And when they neared the house Anzino had been spotted entering, they walked up to the front door as any good visitor would, and knocked on the door. Even Charles found it odd. "I thought the bad guys never knocked," he said. "I thought they always launched a sneak attack out back."

"And the bad guy they're searching for always gets away. You know why?"

"I'm sure you're enlighten me."

"The bad guys are always on to that shit, that's why," Mick responded. "If they're hiding out, they expect the sneak attack. They look for it. They listen for it. They never expect the enemy to boldly knock like some regular Joe. But that's what I rely on. I count on that lack of expectation." He knocked again.

But as soon as he knocked this time, a gunshot could be heard. As soon as they heard it, both men pulled out their loaded weapons. Charles, the bigger of the two men, leaned back and kicked the door open with the leather sole of his leather shoes, and Mick hurried inside, pointing his weapon as he did. Charles, his weapon aimed too, entered behind him. It was a small house, so they were able to see from one end of it to the other end, and they saw the feet of a body hanging out of one of the bedrooms. Then they saw that the backdoor was open.

Mick ran toward the open backdoor, while Charles made his way toward the backroom where the body was lying. As soon as Mick ran out of the backdoor, he saw a figure jump a fence and take off running across a backyard.

Mick ran after him, jumping the fence too. When he landed on his feet, he continued to give chase. But by the time he made it to the next street over, the apparent gunman was jumping into a waiting vehicle, and the vehicle sped away. Mick wasn't close enough to get a license plate, or even to see the make or model of the car, or who the driver was. All he saw was that it was a black boxy car. It could have been a Kia. It could have been a Honda. It could have been a fucking Toyota. He wasn't close enough to say. Dammit!

Then he thought about his brother, who wasn't exactly versed in the ways of the dark side, and hurried back to the yellow house.

Charles made his way down the hall to the room where the feet could be seen. When he saw what he had suspected would be a dead body, undoubtedly the body of Mick's man Anzino, he immediately twirled around, to make sure this was no ambush. Then he checked the other rooms, whipping his gun in first before he stepped in himself. When he saw that the coast was clear, he made his way back to the victim. One gunshot through the forehead. Another life stopped as it appeared to be running into the bedroom for cover. He crossed his chest, said a prayer for the man's soul, and then stepped over his body and entered the room.

He didn't see where the guy was going to find much cover in there, unless he had planned to jump out of the window. Because all he could see was a small bedroom, with a bed, a nightstand, and a chest of drawers. The room was too small for a dresser.

"You okay?"

Charles turned to the sound of Mick's voice. Mick was back, and was staring at the dead man.

"Anzino, I take it?" Charles asked.

"That's that motherfucker," Mick said.

"You think his assailant followed us here?"

Mick nodded and looked at his brother. "That's what I'm thinking, yeah. We went in through the front. He went in through the back."

"And that poor guy," Charles said, "didn't see any of us coming."

"That's what he gets for two-timing his boss," Mick said. "Poor guy my ass. But fuck it. Let's get out of here. He's no help to us now."

"Why do you think he did it?" Charles asked as he began walking back across the room.

"Money," Mick said, glancing back at Charles. "What the fuck else?"

Charles knew Mick had the hardest edge of any man he'd ever met hands down. Even when he was a kid there was something unfeeling about Mick. But it still unnerved him when he saw it. Was he this way with his children? With his *wife*?

And it was then, as Charles was leaving, did he glance at the pictures on the wall of the bedroom. It looked like family pictures. Pictures of ladies, of children, of a dog. But it was one picture that caught Charles's eye. A familiar looking face.

Mick saw his sudden shift in interest. "What?" he asked him.

Charles moved up to the picture, and when he saw it closer, he knew he was right. "*Got*damn," he said.

"What?" Mick asked, walking over to the picture too. All Mick saw was a picture of some short, stocky man with blotchy pink skin.

"Do you know this guy?" Charles asked.

Mick looked closer. "No. Why?"

Charles grabbed the picture off of the wall and turned it over. *Gooch DeCarlo* was written on the back. *August 3, 2010*.

"What of it, Charles?" Mick asked. "What does that ugly fuck have to do with anything?"

"He was younger here. But he's the guy."

"What guy?"

"This ugly fuck is the political agitator who called himself Abe Norris. This ugly fuck is the fucker who shot my wife."

Mick looked at Charles, stunned. Charles looked at Mick. "This is the guy we need to find."

"Don't worry," Mick said. "We're find him."

Sirens could be heard in the distance. Charles kept the photograph, as he and Mick hurried away from the scene.

CHAPTER NINETEEN

Over the next several weeks, life settled back down and they all attempted to resume their normal lives. Mick returned to Philadelphia and his massive corporation. Charles and Jenay returned to Jericho and their business obligations. And all the speculation that once swirled around the discovery of Ethan Campbell's body began to ebb even in Boston. The police determined that his body had been moved from a different location, an outdoors location, and planted at Carly's former house. They concluded he had not been killed in that house, and the person who once lived there, Carly Sinatra, was not involved in the crime.

Although Trevor went back to Boston the same night he had dinner with Carly, to Carly's pleasant surprise, he stayed in touch with her. He stayed in touch practically every single night. Their conversations began with him attempting to get her back on his payroll, but over time devolved into more personal discussions. They talked about their likes and dislikes. They talked about their dreams. They talked about irrelevant things. They enjoyed each other's conversation.

And despite her family's doubts about Trevor, and her father still had many, Carly quickly lost all doubt. Mainly because she knew Trevor before that night with Ethan, but also because, during all of their daily conversations, Trevor never once mentioned anything about Ethan's death or her involvement in it. Life was changing for Carly. She felt as if she had passed some grand test and was now on her way. Life was good.

And then they found Gooch DeCarlo, and everything changed again.

It was almost a month after Carly's arrest. Charles and Jenay were sitting out on the patio, seated side by side on the lounger, when the call came in. Charles was leaned back asleep, his sunglasses covering his eyes, while Jenay was sitting up polishing her toenails.

Robert came out from inside the house carrying an IPhone. "Dad," he said as he entered talking, "you left this on the table." Then he saw the state of his father. "He's sleep?"

Jenay looked at Charles, and then at Robert. "Seems that way to me," she said, and then continued to do her toenails.

"What do I tell Uncle Mick?" Robert asked.

Jenay looked up again. "Mick is on the phone?"

"Yeah. He wants to speak to Dad."

Jenay reached for the phone. Robert handed it over. "Hello, Mick?"

"Jenay, hey. Is Charles there?"

"Yes. But he's asleep. Is it urgent?"

Mick didn't mince words. "Yes," he said.

Jenay knew Mick was not a frivolous man. If he said it was urgent, then she knew it was urgent. She leaned back and shook Charles. "Babe," she said. "Babe!"

Charles opened his eyes quickly, let her words digest, and then looked at her.

"Telephone," she said.

Charles frowned. She woke him up to take a phone call?

"It's Mick," she quickly added, before he jumped on her case.

Charles, knowing Mick did not call to chew the fat, accepted his cell phone from her. "What's up?" he asked.

"I have your agitator."

"Where? In Philly?"

"Boston. He finally came out of his cave when he thought the heat was off. Want me to fly up and get you?"

"That'll be faster," Charles said.

"I'm on my way," Mick said, and they ended the call.

"What's wrong, Dad?" Robert asked.

"Just a situation," Charles said, and looked at Jenay.

"You've got to go?" Jenay asked.

"Yup."

"They found him?"

Charles nodded. "Yup," he said. Then he leaned against Jenay, which she knew meant he was still tired, and kissed her on the lips. Then he got up.

"Can I go with you, Dad?" Robert asked. He was out of the loop, and badly wanted in.

Charles looked at Robert. He hated that his oldest boy Brent was involved in this mess. Not Bobby too. "No," he said firmly, as he made his way into the house.

Gooch DeCarlo sat in the chair against the wall. Three men guarded him, and one stood at the window. But all were heavily armed.

"They're here," said one, as he left the window and walked over to the door. He waited to hear a knock, and then opened the door.

Mick and Charles walked in like two well-dressed enforcers from way back. Already Charles knew this wasn't going to be as simple as interrogating the guy and letting him go. The guy, this Gooch, had already been worked over royally. He was so badly beaten that his forehead had a tennis ball-size hickie on it, and his left eye was swollen shut.

Mick stood in front of Gooch, and then knelt down. Gooch leaned back reflexively when he realized Mick the Tick was in front of him. Charles stood behind his younger brother. This was not his element, he was no gangster, but he had Mick's back.

"My driver betrayed me," Mick said. "My question is why?"

Gooch knew he was already dead. Mick the Tick didn't come to these hellholes to show mercy. Gooch wasn't going to feign ignorance the way he knew most men in a tough spot like his would do. He was going to show something he knew Mick hated: disrespect. "Do I know you?" he asked him.

"You stupid fuck!" one of Mick's men said to Gooch.

"Want me to show him how well he knows you, boss?" another one of Mick's men asked.

"Is that necessary, Gooch?" Mick asked. When Gooch didn't respond, Mick reached into his pocket and pulled out what appeared to be a hand-sized grabber. But instead of hitting the guy, Mick took the grabber and latched it onto

Gooch's crotch. He squeezed. Gooch screamed. "Is it necessary, Gooch?" he asked again.

Even Mick's men looked away when that grabber latched onto the man's balls. Charles wanted to look away too, but he knew Mick was pumping the guy for information, and he was doing it for Carly's sake. For Charles's daughter's sake. He wasn't about to look away.

Gooch didn't look away either. He was too busy screaming out in agony and pain.

"You still haven't answered my questions, Gooch," Mick said as he continued to squeeze. "You still haven't told me if I should put my boys on you again." Mick squeezed harder. "You still haven't told me why my pea brain of a motherfucking driver thought it made sense to betray me."

Gooch was still screaming and his face was fire red as he lifted in his seat and tried with every muscle in his body to break away from Mick's grasp. Mick's men had to look then, when they saw Gooch's attempts at freedom. But it was still painful to see.

"Why, Gooch?" Mick asked again, as he squeezed again and then twisted.

"Damn!" one of Mick's men said and completely backed up. He touched his own balls, as if by abstention Gooch's troubles spelled trouble for him.

"Money," Gooch finally said, breathlessly, and Charles, pleased that he was now willing to talk, unfolded his big arms.

Mick released the grabber. "Money?" Mick asked him.

Gooch let out a sharp exhale when Mick released him. "Money. He wanted money."

"Why?"

Gooch knew he was a dead man talking, but he couldn't take the kind of torture Mick was putting him through. And with the pain came a grappling at straws. He was irrational now. He actually thought, by talking, he could somehow prolong his life. Or at least give him time to come up with another implausible way out. "I do jobs," he said. "That's how I make my living. No matter how big or small, I do jobs. So I was asked to keep an eye on Carly Sinatra."

Charles's jaw tightened. Mick's did too. "Who asked you?" Mick asked.

"Don't know. It was a blind run. All bank transactions. They paid like they were supposed to pay, and I did what I was supposed to do. I kept an eye on her. When she went home for the night, that was the end of my day."

He paused, as the pain continued to inflict him. "Then Ethan Campbell went missing. Word around the Boston underworld was that Mick the Tick had been in town the night Ethan disappeared. But nobody knew anything conclusive. I was paid to get one of your men to flip, to give me intel on what you were up to that night. But I got nothing. I couldn't even get those fuckers to confirm if you were even in town. I got no takers. So they sent me to Jericho, to volunteer for the Cruikshank campaign."

"Cruikshank's involved?" Charles asked.

"Hell no. He was just a way in. My job was to agitate, to incite the locals to turn against you, same as Cruikshank was preaching in his campaign. It was all about bringing you down," Gooch said, looking at Charles. "It was all about destroying you."

He paused again, as the pain continued to rip through his body. "Then I get this call from Anzino. He says he was your driver the night Ethan went missing. He said he not only knew where the body was, but where they took the body from. I should have contacted my employer. They had a contact I was supposed to check in with in Jericho, and I should have done so. Their mission for being in Jericho was the same as mine: to get intel that could destroy you too. But I didn't go that route. I saw Anzino's call as my chance. He wanted five mill and a ticket out of the country, so I would ask for ten mill. Five apiece. Only person I knew could get that kind of money was you." He was nodding toward Mick. "But it wasn't enough for me to just tell you I knew where the body was buried. I needed a weapon against you."

"What kind of weapon?" Mick asked.

"Carly," Gooch said. "So me and Anzino and a few good men I paid, went and dug up that body and put it right back where Anzino said your men got it from: Carly's house. We had already found out the house was still empty. We already knew nobody, after Carly left those weeks earlier, had rented it out."

"What was the plan?" Mick asked.

"The plan was to put the body there and then call you and tell you, for ten mill, we wouldn't go to the cops and implicate your cute little black niece. But as we were leaving Carly's house that night, we weren't a good four blocks away, there was an ambush. Every last one of my men were killed. I got away. That's what I do. Anzino did too."

Gooch frowned. "I had this safe house nobody knew about, that I went too whenever I was in trouble and needed to hide out. So I went there. Me and Anzino. We didn't know what to do. We couldn't call you. We didn't know if you were the one who ambushed us. We wasn't going to call the cops. What good would that do us? But then the owner of Carly's old rent house, a house that hadn't been rented out, went to the house that next day. Found the body before anybody could do anything about it. And he called the cops. Then the next thing I know your men are on my street scoping out my house. I call for one of my men to meet me on the backstreet, I kill Anzino because I couldn't leave witnesses, and then I took off. I was running out of the back door just as you and your brother were breaking down my front door. And I got away. That's what I do. Until now."

"Who was your Jericho contact?" Charles asked. "You said there was somebody in Jericho you were supposed to answer to. Who was he?"

"A she," Gooch said. "Gilda Lane."

Charles knew that name. "Gilda Lane? The biker chick?"

"Her job was to get cozy with Donnie Sinatra. He was considered the weakest link of your children, the one easiest to con. Her job was to pump him for information, stay close to him, and use him to whatever benefit we needed. She didn't know the big plan either, but she knew more than I did."

Charles was ready. They had what they needed to get to the bottom of this. But Mick had unfinished business. He walked with Charles outside of the front door, and even closed the door, but then he stood still. "Wait in the car," he said to his brother. "I'll be there."

Charles looked Mick in the eyes. He knew what he meant. "He placed that body back in Carly's house. He placed her, my child, in a freedom-threatening situation. It used to be my belief that the law should handle it. I gave up that right when we buried that body. But it will never end, Charles, if we keep burying more bodies."

"That is not true," Mick said. "It never ends the moment you bury your *first* body. It doesn't matter if you do another one or not. It is hellish, and it never ends. But it will for you, and for your family. I'll see to that."

Charles stared at his brother. Mick was younger, but in a lot of ways, even when he was a kid, he was never young. "Is that why you have to go back in?" he asked him.

Mick nodded. "That's exactly why. Going back in is the only way out."

Charles swallowed hard, and nodded. Mick

didn't need his permission, but he appreciated it. He squeezed his big brother's shoulder, and went back inside. Charles knew he could have gone to the car and pretended it wasn't happening. But he was not that kind of man. He stood there and waited. It didn't take long. He expected one gunshot. One should have been enough. He heard five. It reminded him of when Mick was a kid, and the neighborhood children would always complain that he played too rough. That he took it too far. Other men killed. Mick overkilled.

Charles walked away from the house, and got in the car. But it didn't feel triumphant in the least. It didn't feel like a climb to the top, but like a race to the bottom. It felt like another nail banging in another one of his children's coffins.

But if they thought Gilda Lane would roll over like Gooch DeCarlo and tell all she knew, they had another thought coming. As soon as her front door was kicked in, she wasn't running out of any back doors. She ran to her room, grabbed her always loaded, semiautomatic rifle from behind her door, and ran out shooting.

Mick and Charles took cover, but she was no match for either one of them. Mick was about to fire, but Charles took her out with a single bullet through the eye. She stood there momentarily, her rifle still aimed and ready to fire, as if her stubbornness alone would get her out of the jam she found herself in, and then fell backwards.

Mick and Charles stood up again. Mick, upset that Charles didn't let him take the shot instead, exhaled. Mick didn't want his brother to have that death on his conscience. But Charles didn't want it on Mick's either. Charles won out.

But as Mick stared at him, Charles didn't even look his way. He continued to stare at Gilda Lane. "Don't you worry about me, Michello," he said. "I do what I have to do too."

Then Charles looked at his brother. And Mick nodded. For once in his life, he felt as if he and his brother were equals on his terrain.

But when the dust cleared and they cleared out of that house, the fact remained: they were no closer to figuring out who attempted to take Charles down, and Carly and Jenay along with him. Gilda wouldn't let them take her alive. They were back to square one.

CHAPTER TWENTY

A week after Gilda's death, Donald Sinatra was still in shock. Not just because she died. That was bad enough. But because, according to his father and Brent, she was using him for some bigger, political purpose.

"What kind of bigger purpose?" he remembered asking his father.

"She wanted to destroy me," Charles had responded. "She was working for my enemies, and she was out to destroy me."

Donald remembered frowning. "What enemies?" he asked. "You mean like Cruikshank? Why he's just a pompous blowhard!"

"He's on his way to becoming our new mayor, if the polls are right. He's more than a blowhard. But not Cruikshank. Somebody else."

"Who?"

Charles hated to admit it. "We don't know yet. Gilda came out with both barrels blazing and wasn't interested in conversation. We had no choice, son."

Brent handled the case, and didn't press

charges against his father, which only gave more fodder to Cruikshank's campaign a couple months before the election. He had been running for nearly a year. He had been trying to paint Charles as the enemy all that time. Brent's exoneration of his own father proved that the Sinatras were a monopoly that looked out for nobody but themselves, and Cruikshank ran with it. But Brent didn't care. It was self-defense and he was treating it that way. Makayla, as DA, treated it the same way too, despite Cruikshank's calls that both of them recuse themselves.

But Donald was on his family's side. He knew his father wouldn't harm a flea unless that flea was trying to harm his family. Gilda was a hothead. That was why he could never love her the way she wanted him to. He loved her sex, and he was going to miss that about her, but he doubted if he was going to miss *her*. His father said they had no choice, and he believed him. He knew Gilda was the type to shoot first and ask questions later. But when his father said he and Uncle Mick went to talk to her, Donald also knew she was shooting first at two men who wouldn't hesitate to shoot back.

But it still hurt. He still was tired of being used and abused by these women. He was still tired of always picking the wrong kind of girl.

Carly was picking the wrong kind of boy, in her family's eyes, but she decided weeks ago that she couldn't let somebody else determine her life. She knew they didn't trust Trevor. She knew her Uncle Mick believed, without being able to prove it, that he was shady.

But she knew how Trevor treated her. She knew how he phoned her every night and, over the last couple of weekends, how he came to see her. He didn't want anything from her when he came. He just wanted her company. And he never, not once, grilled her about Ethan Campbell or anything about that night. She already had a secret crush on Trevor long before that night. And the fact that he dropped everything to get her out of jail, and his subsequent treatment of her, only heightened her interest in the one man whose presence alone made her happy.

She made herself a bowl of cereal and sat at the island counter beside Donald and Ashley. Both were eating too. "Good morning, people," she said. "Where's Bonita?"

"She spent the night at Brent and Makayla's." Then Donald frowned. "Why are you so cheerful?"

"Because I am. It's Saturday. I don't have to go to work. It's a good day."

"But I have to go to work. It's a lousy day."

"Isn't Saint Cat's having that fundraiser today?" Ashley asked. "That car wash?"

"They're having it," Carly said, "and I should probably be there. But I'm not going."

"You aren't a very good teacher," Donald said. "The teachers I remember were devoted seven days a week. Not just five days a week."

"Perhaps they were. But I'm not."

"Don't pay Donnie any attention," Ashley said. "He's not exactly devoted to his job like that either."

"Yeah, but I'm a natural goof off. She's not. At least not in Dad's eyes."

"Or her own eyes," Ashley added, and Carly laughed.

Donald looked at her with an even stranger frown. "What's funny? That's not funny."

"Don't hate just because you have to go to work," Carly responded. "You should be glad you have a job. Mom doesn't have to work, Dad takes care of her, but she works harder than anybody I know. She works every single Saturday."

"Has she left already?" Donald asked.

"You know she has," Carly said. "She's never late, unlike you. Why are you still here anyway?"

"Ah, put a sock in it, Carly," he responded,

and Carly laughed.

"Now I'm with Donnie," Ashley said. "Why are you so gosh-darn happy?"

"I told you why. I'm off today. It's a good day."

"So what are you going to do?" Ashley asked her. "No. Let me guess! You're going to read books. Then go to the library and read more books. Then come home and watch reruns of *The Big Bang Theory*. Am I right?"

Carly smiled. "Wrong. As usual."

"So what are you going to do?" Ashley asked.

Carly hesitated. Ashley and Donald both looked at her.

"What?" Carly asked.

"You didn't answer my question. What's the big deal?"

"Nothing."

"Then what are you going to do this weekend?"

Carly exhaled. "I'm going to Boston for the weekend."

"You're *what*?" Ashley and Donald asked in unison. "Why would you go to a place like that," Donald asked, "when they tried to pin a murder on you?"

"For real, Car," Ashley said. "You don't need to be going up in that place. Are you nuts?"

"I know why she's going," Donald said. "She's going to see that man. I'll bet any amount of money."

"What man?" Ashley asked.

"The one that came to her rescue in Boston. Her former boss. Trevor somebody."

"Oh, you mean cutie," Ashley said with a smile. "I saw a picture of him. Well," she added, "if he's the reason."

"Ash!" Donald said.

"Don't *Ash* me! A good man is hard to find."

"But he's not good," Donald said. "I overheard Dad and Mom talking. They think that guy is bad news."

"They don't know him," Carly said.

"You don't either!" Donald replied.

"I do know him. I worked for the man, remember?"

"He was your boss. It was purely professional, I'm sure. That was different." He looked at Carly. "Don't do it, Carly."

Carly had had enough. "Just leave it alone, alright?" She stood up and went around to the sink.

Donald leaned against Ashley. "I'll be back," he said, got up, and headed upstairs.

"Dad!" Donald yelled as he entered the bedroom. He heard the shower running and went in the direction of the master bath. The door was open, and he could see the steam coming from the running shower water, but when he entered the bathroom and saw his father's silhouette through the shower stall door, he froze. At first it looked as if his father was humping the shower wall. His back was to the door and his bare ass was pushing up into something, over and over again. If it was a person he was fucking, that person was so small she was virtually invisible. Then Donald saw what appeared to be a slender, shapely leg beside his father's. A woman's leg. His dad wasn't humping the shower stall wall, he was humping a woman. But what woman? His stepmother, Jenay, had already left for work. What the fuck?

Donald moved closer. He was angry now. How could his father betray Jenay like this? And he was going to expose it right here and right now!

Donald flung open the shower stall door angrily. "How could," he started saying when the door flew open. Until his father turned toward him in shock, his penis dropping out of the woman's ass, and he got a tiny glimpse of his stepmother's face as she turned toward him too. That quick glance alone gave Donald an even quicker glimpse of her small, brown ass.

Charles knew it too, and it only inflamed his already hot temper. "Are you out of your *got*damn mind?" he angrily asked his youngest son as he flung the shower door back closed. "What the fuck is wrong with you? You know not to come into our suite without permission!"

"I'm sorry!" Donald said, truly mortified. "I didn't know Mom was still home, I swear. Carly said Mom had already left for work. I didn't know it was Mom!"

"What do you want?" Charles asked in a voice that made it clear he was still super-hot, as he continued to shield Jenay's entire body.

Donald had forgotten what he had wanted. He was as traumatized as they were.

"What, Donald?" Charles asked him again.

"Carly," he said, remembering.

"Carly what?"

"Carly says she's going to spend the weekend in Boston. With that Trevor guy."

Charles's heart dropped. So did Jenay's. "She's *what*?" she asked.

"Where is she?" Charles asked.

"Still downstairs," Donald said. "Having breakfast."

"Tell her I want to talk to her," Charles said.

"She's not to go anywhere until I get down there. I'll be there shortly."

"Yes, sir," Donald said, still mortified. "And I'm sorry, Jenay," he added, as he hurried out of their room.

"That boy!" Charles said as he still held onto Jenay's hips. His penis was no longer inside of her, but had wedged itself between her butt cheeks. She was still turned toward the shower stall wall. "He better not have seen an inch of you," Charles added.

Jenay looked back at him over her shoulder. "I don't think he did," she said. "Your big-ass body had me pretty well covered."

Charles smiled. "I'm not that big."

"I've got news for you, *Big* Daddy. Yes, you are." She rubbed her ass against his penis. "In *every* way."

And that rub did it. Charles began to feel the lust again. He leaned down and kissed her on her mouth, and then turned her around, and kissed her harder.

"What about Carly?" Jenay said as he kissed her.

"She'll wait," Charles said as he lifted her legs against his hips, and guided his penis back into her wet pussy. "She knows not to disobey me."

He pushed into Jenay with a thrust so hard and sensual that she let out a guttural cry. And then he was pumping into her again. She lifted her hands over her head and splayed them against the back of the wall as her body bounced with his every stroke. She was feeling it again too, in a powerful way, as his hands cupped her ass and pumped her even harder.

Charles squeezed her ass as he pumped her. He loved this woman and he loved making love to this woman. And he wanted to show her how much. He was leaving it all on the field. He pushed into her, and pushed into her, until his balls were slapping against her. He leaned down and put her nipple in his mouth, as he fondled, sucked, and bit her.

Jenay let out another cry of joy when he bit her. She was going to have the scars to prove this fuck, and she loved when he went all out. He was holding nothing back. So she didn't either. She lifted his mouth from her breast, and began kissing him. She kissed him as hard as he fucked her. She forgot about every trouble they had in this world, and enjoyed every inch of her man.

She came first, the way he liked it, and stopped kissing him when her orgasm heightened. She began trembling and arching and her face lifted upward. Charles encouraged her. When she said she couldn't bear it, he made her bear it. When she said it was too intense, he banged her harder and made it more intense. Jenay could take it. He knew she could. And Jenay took it. She took everything he threw at her. He pumped his ass off, and she enjoyed the ride.

She enjoyed it so much that it made him cum too. He clenched his teeth and splayed his own hands against the stall as he pushed her back against the wall to hold her up. He pushed deep into her and stayed there, to slow down the intensity of his own ejaculation, but like Jenay, there was no way to stop this train. He came hard. He poured into her and began fucking her again.

He fucked her so hard that Jenay began to climax again too. She wrapped her hands around his neck and slid her back up and down along the wall as he pounded her. They leaned into each other and kissed each other as the feelings gave them the release they loved. Even the bone of her thighs felt the tremble.

And when they were done, and could feel their strength begin to collapse around them, they leaned against each other for support. She held him up, and he held her up. And he looked her in the eyes. "We've been together a long time, Jenay," he said. "How can it possibly keep being this good?"

Jenay smiled. "Maybe this time is as good as it gets," she said.

But Charles was shaking his head. "No, baby," he said. "We thought that the last time, remember? And the time before that. And the time before that."

Jenay laughed. "I get your point," she said.

Charles's look turned serious. "I never thought love was meant for a man like me. I never thought I believed in this kind of love. All I've ever known of relationships was abject failure, beginning with my own. To have a lady like you means everything to me, Jenay. Thank you for being a part of my life. Thank you for being a part of my children's life. Sometimes I just need to say thank you."

Jenay's heart swelled with emotion. "Thank you, Charles, for restoring my faith in love too. You were cynical, but so was I. Until you came along. Thank you."

Charles pulled her into his arms. He was drained and weak as hell, but he held onto Jenay. He had matters to attend to, not least of which was Carly, but he held onto the one person who gave him the strength to stand. Everybody had to wait when it came to Jenay.

CHAPTER TWENTY-ONE

When Charles finally put on his bathrobe and made his way downstairs, Carly had been waiting far longer than she had ever intended to. She was a grown woman. This was her life. What was there to talk about?

Plenty, in Charles mind. He tied his robe as he made his way toward the kitchen.

"Uh-oh," Donald said, whispering to Ashley. "Dad's here."

"Hey, Dad," Ashley said.

Charles walked over by her and gave her a hug. "Hey, baby," he said. Then he headed toward the coffeemaker to pour himself a cup of coffee.

Carly looked at him. She was seated at the center island on the opposite side of Ashley and Donald. She turned back toward her father. "You wanted me to wait?" she asked.

Charles began pouring coffee into his mug. "Where are you going?"

"I'm sure Dutiful Donnie already told you."

"Where are you going?" Charles asked again.

Carly realized who she was dealing with and stopped with the sly remarks. "Boston," she said. "For the weekend."

"That's not happening," Charles said

bluntly as he grabbed his cup and made his way beside her at the island.

"Why not, Daddy?" she asked. "I'm only going for the weekend. It's no big deal."

"Just because there's been a passage of time," he said, "doesn't mean it's over."

Carly knew he was talking about how close she came to being arrested for Ethan's murder. She also knew it was about Trevor too. "What do you have against him?" Carly asked. "What does Uncle Mick and all of his minions have against him? What have they found? Nothing, right? That's why Uncle Mick sent his bodyguards away. Because there's nothing to guard. Trevor comes to town and sees me. We enjoy good conversation. And he leaves. That's the beginning and end of it. But yet I'm supposed to treat him like a pariah on some hunch you might have."

But Charles saw it a different way. Anzino, Gooch DeCarlo, and Gilda Lane were all dead, but somebody was behind the scenes pulling the strings. This shit wasn't over by a longshot, as far as Charles was concerned. "It's one thing for that man to come to Jericho and spend time with you," he said to Carly. "That's fine. You're in your element. You're around your family. But you aren't going to Boston. Not yet."

"Then when can I go? When is this going to end? Never? Are you going to always have your suspicions about him?"

"I might," Charles said.

"But based on what?" Carly asked in a flustered voice. "You have no proof, Daddy."

Charles looked at Carly. She had every logical explanation. But this wasn't about logic. This was about his gut feeling that something wasn't right about that Trevor Reese. "You aren't going to Boston to spend not a day, not a weekend, not any time with that man. Do I make myself clear?"

But Carly wouldn't answer. Donald and Ashley looked at her. "You should listen to Dad," Ashley said. "He's only looking out for you."

"I can look out for myself," Carly said.

"Not when it comes to men, you can't," Donald said. "You think you can, but you don't know what they're really up to. Like Gilda. I had no clue she was using me to get to Dad. But she was. What if this Trevor person is doing the same thing?"

"The election is coming up," Ashley said. "Maybe Trevor Reese works for Cruikshank."

"Yeah," Donald echoed.

But Carly frowned and shook her head. "You don't know what you're talking about!

261

Trevor wouldn't be working for some small town political hack like Cruikshank."

"You don't know who he might work for," Donald said. "He could be a serial killer for all you know."

"Oh for crying out loud!" Carly decried.

"Donnie's right," Ashley said. "Or maybe he's a big time drug dealer and your stupid ass is walking right into his trap. You need to listen to Dad, Carly."

"You need to forget that loser," Donald said, "and get yourself a boozer."

Carly looked at him as if he was nuts. "What?"

"At least a drunk is honest," Donald clarified. "At least a drunk wants to make love not war."

"Speak for yourself," Ashley said. "I know plenty drunks who want to make both."

"Will you two knock it off?" Carly asked. "This is my life, not yours, and I'll live it anyway I damn well please! And if that includes me going to spend a weekend with a man I happen to enjoy spending time with, then that's what it shall include. Nobody is going to tell me how to live my life. Just as I wouldn't deign to tell either of you how to live yours! This is my life," Carly continued with emotion she didn't expect to display, "and I'm tired of being told how to live it."

Jenay came downstairs, tying her bathrobe. The loud voices caused her to come. She headed for the kitchen. Everybody were staring at Carly.

"Ever since I was a child I've been forced to do what everybody else wanted me to do," Carly continued. "I made all A's in high school because that's what everybody expected me to make. I went to Harvard because that's where I was expected to go. I graduated with high honors because I was expected to graduate that high. But I'm tired of it now."

Jenay stared at Carly as she walked over by Charles.

"I'm tired of living up to somebody else's image," Carly continued. "I'm tired of doing what somebody else expects me to do. It's my turn now. It's my time to live my life the way I want to live it. And if that doesn't meet with any of your expectations, then tough. None of you have always met with mine either. I'm done."

Carly rose to leave. She was that determined. But there was just one problem with her escape plan: her father.

Charles grabbed her by the wrist, and pulled her back. "I told you already," he said, "and I'm going to tell you again. You are not going to Boston."

"I have to go!" Carly angrily yelled.

Charles frowned. "Why do you have to go?" he yelled back.

"Because it's what I want to do for a change. It's what *I* want, not you!"

"What do you want, Carly?" Charles asked her. "Trevor Reese? You actually think that man wants you?"

Jenay could tell there was a kink in Carly's armor. She could tell Carly wasn't all that certain of Trevor's true feelings for her.

"What he wants," Carly responded to her father, "isn't the point."

"Well it damn well better become the point," Charles said. "Because you don't know what you're getting yourself into. At least you need to know that he's worth it. At least you need to know that he loves you and is willing to go through the fire with you the way you're willing to go through it with him."

"Mom came to Jericho to be with you on faith," Carly said. "She wasn't sure if you really loved her. She told me so herself. But she had to try. All I'm doing is trying for my life's sake. Love isn't a guarantee. It's never been and never will be."

"That's true," Jenay said, and everybody looked at her. "But Charles wasn't back then and has never been some mystery man I couldn't learn shit about. He's never been shady like that. You can't compare your father to a man like Trevor Reese."

"I'm not trying to compare them," Carly said. "I'm just trying to see if it will work."

"And what if it doesn't work?" Charles asked. "Is it worth the price you might pay? What if he doesn't even want you like that?"

"I'm sure he wants me," Carly said, although it was with weak conviction. "He wants me," she said with more forcefulness.

"But he wants you for what, Carly?" Charles asked. "To be his woman, or to be his whore?"

Carly couldn't believe her father spoke those words to her. And she slapped him. She slapped Charles hard across his face.

Donald and Ashley jumped to their feet in shock, holding each other's arms. "Oh, snap!" Ashley yelled. "Call Rescue, Donnie, call Rescue! Daddy about to kill this crazy girl!"

But Charles didn't have time to do anything to Carly. Jenay stepped in between them and did it for him. She slapped Carly even harder across her face.

When Carly looked back up, holding the side of her now stinging face, she saw a kind of fierceness in Jenay that she had never seen before.

"Don't you ever," Jenay said between clenched white teeth, "even think about raising your hand to your father ever again! He's your father. This man right here! The one who brought you into his family and loved and cared for you like you were his own flesh and blood. The one who sacrifice for you time and time again no matter what the problem may be. I don't care what words come out of his mouth, I don't care how much you hate those words, he is your father! And you will respect that."

Carly looked at her mother, and then looked at her father, and she knew she was wrong. She regretted what she had just done, she regretted it with bitter regret. She looked back at her father, and tears appeared in her eyes. "Daddy, I'm sorry," she said heartfelt.

To Donald and Ashley's total shock, tears appeared in Charles's eyes too. And when Carly fell against him, and hugged him, they were equally shocked when he hugged her back.

Jenay wasn't shocked. She was grateful. Because Charles knew like she knew that there was more going on with Carly than meets the eye. There was more pain and hurt inside of that young woman than she would ever reveal.

Carly looked at Jenay as she held Charles, with her tears still dropping freely, and she pulled Jenay into her embrace too. And apologized to Jenay too.

But as Carly held her parents, she knew it wasn't enough. She knew they weren't listening to her. They weren't trying to feel the pain she'd been feeling practically all of her life, because it would be unimaginable to good, God-fearing people like them. She had no voice. She had no say in her life. She was screaming, but nobody was hearing her. She was crippled by other people's expectations, and they couldn't see the crutches. She was paralyzed by other people's wants and needs, and they couldn't see the paralysis. She had to walk away. Didn't they understand that? She was a paralyzed woman trying to walk away. She knew she had no business walking at all, not a woman in her condition. But she *had* to try.

After her embrace of her parents ended, and it was clear that they had accepted her apology, she moved away from them and began heading upstairs.

Jenay turned toward her. "Where are you going?" she asked.

"To change," Carly responded. "They're having a car wash at Saint Cat's." Then she swallowed hard. It was a bitter pill to swallow. "They expect me to be there," she added, and hurried upstairs.

Charles looked at her as she left the room. Donald and Ashley looked at him, surprised that he didn't run Carly down and knock her through a wall. But they didn't see anger in their father's eyes. They saw pain. Tremendous pain. Jenay looked at him. She saw it too.

"I've got to get ready for work," Charles said, and left. He headed upstairs too.

Jenay exhaled. She could just feel his agony.

Donald and Ashley, however, could only feel their own. "I told you," Donald said. "Carly gets away with everything. If that had been me or Ash who slapped Dad like that, we'd be on the floor."

"They wouldn't even have to call Rescue," Ashley agreed.

"That's right," Donald said, nodding his head. "Because we would have already been dead! Dad would have killed us on the spot. I told you, Ma. You think we be lying. But I told you. Carly gets away with murder!"

Jenay looked at Donald and Ashley as if they knew about that night in Boston. She looked at them as if they had just revealed the great secret of the universe. And then she realized who she was talking about. Donald and Ashley. Both of them together wouldn't have brains enough to reveal their own secrets, let alone somebody else's. "Boy, if you don't leave me alone," she said to Donald, and headed upstairs too.

CHAPTER TWENTY-TWO

Jenay stopped her Mercedes in front of Charles storefront office building, grabbed her paperwork, and got out. She hurried across the sidewalk, speaking to a passerby, as she entered the building.

Her stepson Robert was there, sitting on the edge of the desk of one of the clerks, running his hand through his thick, blond hair and making her laugh at his dirty jokes. He smiled when he saw Jenay. "Hey, Ma," he said. "I heard there were fireworks at the house this morning."

"Is he in?" Jenay asked.

"He's in. But he's in a nasty mood. He told us that he doesn't want to be bothered. With no exceptions, he said."

Jenay headed straight for his office.

"Of course he didn't mean you," Robert said out of earshot of Jenay, and the ladies in the office laughed.

Jenay heard the laughter but didn't care what it was about. Charles was on her mind. And their daughter. She knocked once on his closed office door, and entered.

Charles was seated behind his desk, but his back was to the door. He was looking out of his window.

Jenay walked slowly into the office, and then walked around to the window. He didn't react, as if he knew it was her all along. He just continued to stare.

"Carly's at Saint Catherine's," he said.

Jenay didn't expect him to say that. "You went there?"

"I saw her. She's where she said she was going to be. And when I drove up, to get my car washed, guess what she did?"

Jenay braced herself. "What? She continued to argue with you? She cussed you out? What?"

"She smiled as if nothing had happened. She's still wearing that *got*damn mask, Jenay." He looked at his wife. "And I can't do a damn thing about it!"

Jenay let out a harsh exhale. "I found something, Charles," she said.

Charles, leaned back in his chair, looked at her. "What?"

Jenay handed him the folder that was in her hand. "That's Trevor Reese's client list for his marketing firm. The list Mick's man gave to you."

"Yeah, so?" He began thumbing through

the paperwork in the folder.

"Look on page seven."

Charles looked. "Okay," he said. "What am I looking for?"

"Go to the F's," Jenay said.

He did. At first he didn't see it. Then he did. He leaned forward. "Sharon Flannigan," he said, and then looked at Jenay. "Where do I know that name?"

"Oh, Charles, don't you remember? She's the new Headmistress at Saint Catherine's."

Charles stood to his feet. "And she's on Reese's client list?"

"And she was in the lobby when that agitator fired those shots," Jenay said.

For the first time in weeks, Charles felt as if they were getting somewhere. "Where is she? At that car wash?"

"No, she just got back to the Inn. I saw her go to her room just before I discovered this. I didn't know how to approach her. I came to you."

"You did right, baby," Charles said, squeezing her arm. "Let's go," he added, as he grabbed his suitcoat off of the back of his chair, and hurried out.

"She left, you know."

Carly was standing there in a pair of shorts

and a tucked-in shell top. She wasn't washing cars, because they had more than enough students present to handle that. She, instead, spent most of her time standing around and thinking.

"You heard me, Carly?" It was Marge, one of her fellow teachers. They were standing in the parking lot of the Saint Catherine's Prep Academy as a dozen students washed a steady flow of cars.

"You heard me, Carly?"

"What is it?" Carly asked.

"Our Headmistress. She left already. I know she didn't have to be here at all, just as we don't have to be. But it's about supporting the students. She could have at least stayed until the end of the day." She looked at Carly. "Don't you agree?"

Carly thought about it. "No," she said, and looked at Marge.

Marge was surprised. "No? Why would you say no?"

"She's not needed here. The kids are washing the cars. The vestry's hand-picked chaperones are handling the traffic and the money. Why should she have to stand out here all day? Why should we?"

Marge was confused. "To prove that we're supportive," she said.

"But to prove it to whom? The students? They don't care. The Headmistress? She doesn't care."

"To prove it to ourselves then."

"To prove what to ourselves, Marge?" Carly asked.

Marge was flustered. It wasn't something she had ever thought about. "I don't know. It's expected of us to be here, if we're good teachers. Why are you asking me such questions? I do what I'm told."

And that was when it hit Carly. Once again, she was doing what was expected of her. Not what she wanted to do. Not even what other people wanted her to do. But what she *assumed* they wanted her to do. She wasn't even doing what she was told, as Marge put it, but what she *assumed* they wanted to tell her to do. She was being good Carly all over again. Going above and beyond. Being Miss Perfect, as Donald and Ashley sneeringly called her. And she was unhappy. And nobody cared.

She looked at her fellow teacher. "Goodbye, Marge," she said, and began walking away.

"You're leaving already too? I thought we were going to stay until the end of the day. Carly? *Carly*?"

But Carly had already tuned her, and

everybody else, out. She walked to her VW Beetle, out of the shop and good to go, got in, and took off. It was Saturday. She had no husband, no children to get home to. She was going to do what she wanted to do for a change.

Tony Sinatra saw her as soon as he walked into the Inn. He came by to say hey to his stepmother, which he often did, but when he saw Sharon eating her dinner in the restaurant inside the Inn, he headed in that direction.

Sharon let out a harsh exhale as he approached, which didn't help his confidence, but Tony had a way of shielding himself. He smiled broadly. "Hello, stranger."

Sharon understood the reference. They hadn't seen each other since he came by her hotel room after the shooting. Her choice. "Hello."

"Having dinner, I see."

"Yes."

"May I join you?"

He could tell she didn't want that, but she was in a shell too. He pressed. "I won't bite, I promise," he said.

She smiled. "You may."

Tony sat down across from her.

"Have some?" she asked.

"Between you and me," he said, "I wouldn't eat the food here if my life depended on it."

She looked at him with horror in her eyes.

"No, I'm kidding," he said, and she relaxed. "But I'm good. Not hungry."

Sharon continued to eat.

"I thought you'd be over at the church," Tony said. "At the car wash."

"I was there earlier, but I saw where they had it well in hand."

"So tell me, Miss Flannigan, how have you been enjoying your stay in Jericho so far?"

"I'm still getting my sea legs, but I think I'll be fine. The school needs a lot of changes, but I'm game."

"That's the spirit," Tony said for a smile. "I always figured old Joe Huddleson to be the wrong jockey for a horse like that school, but what do I know?"

"You know more than you give yourself credit for," Sharon said. Then she added: "I listen to your radio program."

Tony smiled. "Oh, yeah? How often?"

She thought about it. "Since I've been in town? Every day," she said.

Tony smiled greatly this time. "Smart girl," he said.

They continued to talk, mainly about his

broadcast, as Jenay and Charles entered the Inn. Jenay saw them before her husband did. "Over there," she said. "Come on."

When Charles saw them, he took the lead walking over to them. Jenay felt it was typical Charles. Always protective even thought she had no reason to fear Sharon. There was reason to believe Sharon was involved with Trevor Reese, and Trevor was involved with how Ethan Campbell's body ended up in Carly's former house, but she didn't fear the woman. At least not yet. But Charles wasn't taking any chances.

Tony smiled when he saw his parents approach. "Dad, Mom. Hey."

Charles and Jenay sat at the table. Tony looked at Sharon. He wondered how she felt about this intrusion.

"You know Trevor Reese," Charles said to Sharon.

Tony didn't understand. He knew who Trevor Reese was. He looked at Sharon. Her expression remained unchanged. "Excuse me?" she asked.

"Trevor Reese," Charles said. "What is your relationship with him?"

"Relationship?" Tony asked. "She doesn't have a relationship with Trevor Reese."

"Sharon?" Jenay asked.

"I know him professionally."

"You're one of his clients?"

"Yes."

"Why?"

"I had an issue in Baltimore. I needed my reputation rehabilitation."

Tony looked at her.

Sharon paused. "I had a relationship with a man I later found out was married. When his wife found out, it devastated her, as you can imagine. It devastated me. But she killed him."

Jenay's heart dropped. "Good Lord," she said.

"And she went to jail," Sharon said. "I was blamed."

Tony stared at her.

"So my Bishop," Sharon continued, "recommended that I go and speak with Mr. Reese. Mr. Reese discussed the matter with my Bishop, after talking with me, and they came back with a proposition. I can either get fired outright, or get demoted and accept an assignment in Maine. Jericho, Maine."

"So Trevor Reese arranged for you to come here?" Charles asked.

She nodded. "Yes, sir."

"Did he say why he suggested that your Bishop send you here?" Charles asked.

"He didn't say why, no."

"What were you supposed to do when you got here?" Jenay asked.

"Work to turn around Saint Catherine's mainly. But he also mentioned that he wanted me to get close to the Sinatras."

Tony was surprised. "Get close to us?" he asked. "Close to us to do what?"

"To spy. To get dirt on any one of you I could. But that was the choice they gave me. I could go to Jericho, spy on the Sinatras, or get fired. I came here."

"But you haven't tried to get close to any of us," Tony said. "Just the opposite."

"That's right," Sharon said. "I couldn't in good conscience spy on people. Especially when I don't know why. I chose to keep my distance."

"Has Reese or any of his people been in touch with you?" Charles asked.

"No, sir," Sharon said. "Nobody."

Charles leaned back. Jenay and Tony looked at him.

"What do you think it means?" Jenay asked.

"What I thought all along," Charles said. "He's up to something."

"Anyway," Sharon said, "I'd better get upstairs. It's been a long day." She stood up. Tony rose too. Sharon looked at Charles and

Jenay. "I assure you, Mr. and Mrs. Sinatra, that I had no intention of spying on anybody."

"And nobody's been in touch with you?" Charles asked her again.

"No, sir. No-one."

"Why would he asked you to do it then," Jenay asked, "if he wasn't going to follow up with you?"

"I don't know," Sharon said.

"Maybe she was the backup plan," Tony suggested. "Maybe Reese would rely on her intel if he needed to. Since he's so close to Carly, maybe he didn't need to."

Charles nodded. "That makes sense," he said.

"But that doesn't," Tony said, looking toward the entrance.

"What doesn't?" Charles asked.

"Uncle Mick's in town."

Charles and Jenay turned around and looked toward the entrance. When they saw Mick heading their way, they were surprised too.

"Have a good evening," Sharon said to them, and Charles rose to his feet.

"I'll walk you to your room," Tony said, and he and Sharon left.

"What in the world are you doing here?" Charles asked Mick with a smile, shaking Mick's hand.

"Hello there," Jenay said.

Mick leaned down and kissed her. "How are you holding up?" he asked.

"I'm good."

"Your arm better?"

"Oh, yes. All better. Thanks for asking."

"You're welcome," Mick said, then Mick looked at his brother.

"What is it?" Charles asked.

"There's a connection," Mick said.

Charles's smile left. "With who?"

"Trevor Reese and me," Mick said.

Charles's heart was hammering. "Sit down."

Mick sat down. Charles did too.

"We just found out that a headmistress here in town, the woman who just left, was asked by Rees to spy on us."

Mick had one sleepy eye, but it managed to stretch. "To spy? Why?"

"She couldn't give an answer. And she wasn't going to do it anyway."

"You're sure about that?"

Charles nodded. "We are. Now tell us about this connection."

Mick leaned back and crossed his legs. "We kept running into brick walls," he said. "We couldn't find anything on Reese. We weren't getting anywhere. So I went back to the drawing board. I ordered my people to cross check every prick I've had to . . . *handle,* and to check them against the name Reese."

"And you got a hit?" Charles asked.

Mick nodded. "I got a hit. One guy I had to put out of his misery, a small time hood I used to run with back in my early days in Philly. It turns out he's related to Reese."

"Related how?" Jenay asked.

"He was his father," Mick said.

Charles was floored. "I'll be damn," he said. "His father?"

"His father. I figure he was after me all along. He wants to avenge his father's death. I have too much security for a direct hit on me. That'll be too risky. He tried to sniff me out through you."

"With that gang that couldn't shoot straight? With Gooch and Gilda."

"Right. And anybody he could use."

"So what happens next?" Jenay looked from Mick to Charles. Charles looked at Mick.

"We pay Mr. Reese a visit," Mick said.

CHAPTER TWENTY-THREE

Trevor Reese handed her a glass of wine and took a seat on the sofa beside her. Carly already felt overwhelmed by the fact that she had come at all, and was still digesting what she saw when she got there.

Trevor saw her troubled look as soon as she entered his home. It was her first time this intimate with him ever. They had grown closer because of their daily conversations, and the few times he was able to get to Maine to see her. But this was her first time coming to Boston to see him. He knew he had to get her to relax. What he had in store for her required it.

He turned his body toward her, and crossed his legs. "What are you feeling?" he asked her. "Tell me your innermost thoughts, Carly."

Carly had so many thoughts until she didn't know where to begin. She turned to him. She was casually dressed, in her shorts and tucked-in shell top. It wasn't her original plan when she made up her mind a few days ago to come to Boston. But after that emotional morning with her parents, and what happened with her father, she canceled those plans earlier. Trevor was disappointed, but he did not pressure her, which she loved.

But when she decided, while standing in that parking lot at Saint Catherine's, that she was going to just drive on over anyway, she didn't bother to check into her hotel and change. Afraid she would change her mind again, Trevor told her to drive straight to his place. He would take her to her hotel later. So she did. She drove straight over. Now she was in her feelings in ways she could hardly verbalize. But he wanted her to do just that.

She looked at him. He was casually dressed too, in a pullover shirt, a pair of black slacks, and with an expensive Rolex on his wrist as the only apparel that revealed his wealth. But his wealth appeared to be extensive. From the looks of his home alone, it was even more extensive than Carly had realized. And with his big, violet eyes and his long, thick black hair that flowed down his back, he looked like a Viking to Carly. Like some exotic superhero. And sexy as hell.

"Tell me, Carly," Trevor insisted. "What are you feeling right now?"

"I feel a little overwhelmed," Carly admitted, "to tell you the truth." She never felt comfortable discussing her feelings. And she still didn't, but she felt she could at least say that much.

Although she smiled when she admitted her feelings, Trevor could tell she was still holding back. "What overwhelms you?" he asked.

"For one thing, you have a beautiful home. It's a palace of a home, but it's very beautiful."

Trevor studied her. "You are not accustomed to beautiful homes?"

Carly laughed. "I am, actually. I have uncles and relatives with grand homes. And my father is no slouch either."

Trevor laughed. "True."

"But," Carly continued, "I'm not so accustomed to being in a beautiful home like this with a man like you who, tonight, looks nothing like the man I'm used to seeing and talking to."

Trevor was puzzled. "How do you mean?"

"I've never in my life seen you dressed in anything but a business suit."

Trevor smiled. "Oh, right."

"I've never seen you so relaxed either. Even when you come to visit me in Jericho, you always look like my old boss. Now you look like

. . ."

Trevor stared at her. "Like what, Carly?"

Carly decided to just say it. "Like my friend," she said.

Trevor was offended that she would refer to him with such a bland characterization. He had enough fucking friends. Why would he need her to be another one? But he also knew Carly. He knew, for her, being here at all was a major step. He was not a patient man, but he suspected all along he would have to be patient with her. But there were limits. "Drink your wine," he said. "I will not appear so intimidating to you after that."

Carly laughed, but she didn't touch the wine. She, instead, sat it on the table in front of them. She was going to remain clear and sober this night.

Trevor saw her hesitation too, and was pleased that she was smart enough to take that precaution. It also made clear that he was going to have to work harder to get her in bed, but he was a big boy. He could handle little Carly.

"Let me show you around," he said as he sat his glass on the table too, and rose to his feet.

Carly grabbed her purse and followed him. But it felt surreal to her. This gorgeous man was walking from room to room showing off his home as if he was a real estate agent making the hard sell. And he was talking up every room as if he was very proud of it. That helped to ease Carly too. Because there was something so down-to-earth about Trevor at this very moment that it surprised her. He never showed her this side of himself before. Not even when he came to visit her on her turf. She liked this side of him best.

But when they made it upstairs, and they walked through the double doors that led into the master bedroom, this visit, their brand new relationship, and what she knew Trevor expected from her, became real. And when Carly saw the big poster bed waiting there, as if it was waiting for the two of them, she stopped in her tracks. Trevor bumped into her.

When he realized she was frozen in place, he put his hands on either side of her small shoulders. Then he leaned his head around, to see her eyes. "Are you alright, Carly?" he asked her.

Carly realized her error, and smiled. "Yes," she said. He removed his hands and she turned toward him. "I was just . . . impressed with the room. It's very beautiful."

"Thank you," Trevor responded, although he sensed far more was at work inside of this beautiful lady. "This room impresses me too. You know why?"

They were within inches of each other. Carly could feel the heat. "No," she said. "Why?"

He moved closer, and placed his hands on her arms. He could smell her fresh scent. He could see the sparkle in her eyes. He wanted this woman, and his patience was already beginning to fail. "This is the room," he said, "where I am going to get to know you better, Carly." He knew he was taking a risk. He knew she could shut down right now. But he felt it was more likely than not that she wouldn't.

And he was right. The last thing Carly was doing was shutting down. She could feel her vagina began to crank up and throb. The job for her was keeping her feelings for Trevor controlled.

"What do you say about that?" he asked her.

"About you getting to know me better?" she asked him.

"Yes," he said. "This is the room where I am going to get to know you in the most intimate way." He began to rub her arms. "And you, my dear, are going to get to know me."

Carly's breathing became labored as he

lifted her chin with his hand and looked into her eyes. "You want that," he said, looking from one eye to the other one, as if he were assessing the strength of her desire. "Don't you?"

Carly swallowed hard. She wanted it. She couldn't recall the last time she wanted a man this badly. But the fact that she was admitting it so blatantly when they hadn't even defined the full nature of their relationship, was putting her in a very vulnerable position. Especially if her father was right and her body might be the only thing he wanted from her. But as she looked into Trevor's eyes, and as his mouth began to move toward her mouth, she decided that it was a risk she was willing to take. "Yes," she said. "I want it."

That was all it took. Trevor leaned down and smothered her mouth with a kiss. A kiss that was supposed to be sweet and simple. He didn't want to scare the girl, after all. But as he tasted her, and realized how sweet to the taste she really was, he couldn't stop. A chaste kiss became a long, passionate kiss that was filled with pinned-up aggression. He placed his hand on the side of her face, and kissed her even longer. He pulled her small body against his big body, and kissed her even longer than that.

And Carly felt it too. She stood there and

experienced a kiss from a man, a kiss that wasn't being forced or thrust upon her, for the first time in her life. And it wasn't disgusting as she thought it would be. It was, with Trevor, quite nice.

It was so nice that she didn't realize he was undressing her until she felt a tug on her shell shirt coming out of her shorts. She opened her eyes and saw that he had already removed his pullover shirt, revealing his bare and very muscular upper body, and was in the process of removing hers.

Carly allowed him to not only lift her shirt over her head, but her bra right along with it. Now she was bare-chested too, and bare-feet as she stepped out of her sandals, and began staring into his eyes. He took the purse she still carried in her hand, and placed it on the table within his reach.

He looked down, at her sizeable, taut breasts, and then into her eyes. But when he looked into her eyes, she could see just how filled with lust he truly was. It turned her on even more.

Trevor Reese had a secret. Contrary to what people thought, he was not a ladies man. Women often voiced their interest in him, some even went to incredible lengths to show their interest, but he kept his distance from all of them. He had his occasional bedmates, when his urges became too strong, but he kept those encounters to a minimum too. His lifestyle demanded it.

But now he was starved for a woman. But not just any woman. He was starved for Carly. He wanted *Carly* badly. And when he saw her beautiful brown breasts sitting so tight and firm as if they were waiting for a man like him, and when he looked into her big, beautiful eyes, his desire turned desperate.

He lifted Carly into his arms, with her back against the door, and began sucking those breasts with a maddening sense of want. Carly raked her hands through his hair as she enjoyed the feelings that his mouth produced in her. Because he was sucking and licking and giving her a feeling she didn't think was possible for her to have. She was arching her back as he moved from breast to breast and sucked her. As he moved from nipple to nipple and licked her.

And then he carried her to his bed. Her leg brushed against the thigh of his pants as he carried her, and she felt the outline of a penis so hard and big she could hardly believe it. She was an experienced woman. Far more experienced than most women alive, given her crazy childhood. But she had never experienced anything like this.

That was why, when Trevor laid her on her back, and began removing her shorts and panties, her eyes trained themselves on his midsection. And even though he still had on his trousers, she could see where they had tented into a bundle so thick and long that she wondered if he had patted himself, as some men were known to do.

But she would have to wait to find out because Trevor, as soon as he saw her full nakedness, dropped to his knees, opened her legs wider, and began experiencing her in a way that made her nearly overcome with joy.

Carly had never had an oral before. Every man that had ever touched her body always went straight for her pussy, putting it in whether she was ready for it or not. It wasn't about her anyway.

But Trevor wasn't in that kind of hurry. Because it was about her. It was about both of them. And despite his heightened desire, despite the wonderful thought that he was about to make love to a woman he actually cared about, he was careful to attend to her needs too. Although, in truth, he was enjoying it probably more than she was. Because of the taste. His tongue had circled around her clit, giving her that feeling of joy. But it had also pushed inside, allowing him to suck in her wetness and her sweetness all at once. He was making love to her pussy with his tongue, and then his entire mouth, and didn't want to stop.

And he didn't stop. He took Carly on a ride that had her squirming in his bed. He looked up and saw her breasts bouncing from her movement, as if she could hardly contain herself, and he went down on her even harder. Until he couldn't wait any longer. He still wanted to go down on her, but all the way.

He stood up and began to unbuckle his belt, and unbutton and unzip his pants. Carly was still reeling from the intensity of his oral, but she was not so imbued with passion that she could not look at that bundle she had been dying to see. When Trevor dropped his pants and briefs, and revealed that he was not patted at all, and she saw his long, thick penis spring out in vivid color, she couldn't help it. She actually licked her lips!

Trevor cheered inside. She couldn't imagine what that did to him. The fact that she was so anxious for him to put it inside of her that she could taste it, made his day. He knew he had to put on a condom, he was never going to be so reckless as to make her ever feel that insecure, but he couldn't just yet. He got on top of her and wrapped her into his arms. He needed to hump her first. He needed to feel his bare penis against her bare body, even if it was only surface deep.

Carly's eyes became hooded when she felt that rod against her nakedness. She wanted to jump for joy when he wrapped her in his arms as he rubbed against her. She knew she was going to stop him if he tried to enter her raw, but she was enjoying it this way too. And when he began kissing her again, while he humped her, she closed her eyes and experienced a feeling that she had never felt before. She was on a natural high that was so intense that it felt drug-induced.

He stopped kissing her and looked into her face. His rubbing was becoming even more passionate, and his penis, to her shock, was growing even larger. She opened her eyes as he began rubbing her cheeks and her chin. And when his fingers rubbed her lips sensually, she still felt that wonderful feeling.

But then his fingers gave way to his full hand, and his hand inadvertently covered her mouth. As soon as it did, she saw flashes of all those men from her childhood covering her mouth. And Ethan Campbell's hand covering her mouth. And her biological father's hand covering her mouth. And she couldn't take it. It was happening again. It was happening again!

"*No!*" she cried and pushed Trevor's body off of her. It took all the strength she had, but she pushed him completely off. And jumped out of his bed.

Trevor was floored. "Carly, what's wrong?" he asked, his handsome face a mask of concern and confusion.

But Carly wasn't confused. She was determined. She ran to her purse and pulled out her small pistol. Trevor stood up shocked, as she pointed the gun at him.

"Stay where you are," she said in a trembling, high-pitched, terrified voice. "My father taught me how to use it. Stay where you are!"

What Carly didn't realize was how badly she was shaking as she held the gun. She didn't realize the fear Trevor saw in her big, expressive eyes. And with his hands outstretched, he began walking toward her.

"I said stay where you are, Trevor! I'll kill you! I tell you I will!"

But he wasn't as convinced as she was. He continued to walk toward her. He was less concerned with the fact that she went from making love to him to pointing a gun at him in no time flat, as he was for the reason for this sudden shift. "Give it to me, Carly," he said.

"You aren't shooting anyone."

"But I will!" she said. She was crying now. "I will!"

By the time Trevor arrived at her side, he easily grabbed the tiny gun from her. He held her by her small arms, and stared frowningly into her eyes. "What's the matter with you?" he asked her. There was a sincere need to know, and Carly saw it.

But she couldn't verbalize what she felt. She couldn't put into words the flashes of pain that had haunted her most of her life. She just broke down.

Trevor pulled her into his arms and held her. Feeling his arms around her with love rather than aggression gave her courage. And after several moments of nothing, she spoke. "I never did it," she admitted to Trevor, "without being forced to."

Trevor couldn't believe his ears. He pulled back and looked at her. The anguish on her face broke his heart. "You mean raped?" he asked.

Carly nodded her head. "When you put your hand over my mouth, it brought back so many memories. I thought . . . I thought you. . . I thought. . ." She looked at him. "Not even my family knows," she said.

Trevor felt a swell of emotion that almost

did him in. And he pulled her back into his arms. *Good Lord*, he thought. This poor girl! No wonder he always felt as if she was imprisoned somehow, and wouldn't walk free even though the doors were open, and she could.

He lifted her naked body into his arms. "Don't you worry, my sweet Carly," he said to her. "Nobody will ever force you again."

He carried her to his bed, pulled back the covers, and put her to bed. He was going to sleep in a different room. He was going to give her space, and peace.

But when he was about to move away, Carly took his hand, and pulled him back. "Don't leave me," she said so heartfelt that he felt her pain to the roots of his hair. He sat her pistol on his nightstand, and got in bed with her. And pulled her into his arms.

For the first time in his life, he held a woman in bed without fucking her. For the first time in his life, he held a woman in his bed and actually hoped, not that she would be gone by morning, but that he could hold her forever.

CHAPTER TWENTY-FOUR

Charles and Mick entered Trevor Reese's home on the backside of the large estate. They had silencers on their guns, and had to kill four bodyguards before they made it inside. But they made it in.

Charles, a developer, had obtained the home's blueprints, and had studied them carefully, and led the way across the downstairs. They had night scopes on their weapons, just in case they ran into any dark corners, and cameras, in case they had anyone attempt to ambush from behind, as they checked room by room and made their way up the stairs. Mick took the lead up the stairs. This was nowhere near his first rodeo, and he was prepared for the unexpected.

Upstairs, in the master bedroom, Carly was still in Trevor's arms, the room was dark, and she was fast asleep. Trevor's eyes were closed too, but he was thinking about Carly. He knew she was Sinatra's niece when he hired her to run his PR department. That was the main reason she got the job. For leverage in the future if he needed it.

But that was before he worked with Carly. And got to know the kind of person she truly was. Over time, he found that he actually liked her. He liked her work ethic and her intelligence and her strength of purpose. And just as her heart caused him to change his mind about keeping all women at bay and take a chance on her of all people, her spirit and decency caused him to change his mind about using her as some pawn in the very serious war he was soon to undertake with her Uncle Mick. Trevor actually cared for Carly. It was not love in any traditional sense, as he was convinced he could not love anybody, and he was not going to pretend that was what he was feeling right now. But as he held this beautiful, naked, fragile woman in his arms, he was equally convinced that Carly could take him closer to love than he ever thought possible. Even that was a heady realization for a man like Trevor.

Then he heard a squeak, as if someone was walking up his stairs. It was so slight that it was barely registerable. But he heard it and opened his eyes. What kept him alive all these years was his instinct. And his instincts were telling him to act. Even on that flimsy sound, act. And he did. He pressed the button on his side table, and alerted his in-house guards.

Downstairs, in the basement, his guards saw the flashing red light. It was big and prominent and could not be missed. And within seconds the contingent, some four men strong, were armed with silencers on their guns too, and were running up to the main floor of the Reese estate. They ran across the downstairs, and then up the stairs toward the master bedroom where the alarm had been sounded.

They saw two men just as they were about to enter the master bedroom. And they began firing. But not before Mick and Charles, their cameras already detecting trouble from behind, had already turned and was firing on them.

And while Mick and Charles were in a gun battle with his advancing army of men, Trevor had already jumped out of bed onto the other side of his nightstand, and had already secured his loaded gun, and Carly's tiny pistol too, just in case. He was ready for them.

Mick and Charles took out the four men easily, without either one of them getting hit, but they knew the real action was in the bedroom, where Trevor Reese could be found. And they knew he was undoubtedly armed and ready. Their goal had been to take him alive, to make sure they weren't taking out an undercover FBI operative, but they had been met with too much resistance to fulfill that goal. Now, they knew, they were in a fight for their lives.

Trevor began firing at the intruders, unaware of who they were, as soon as they entered his bedroom. The Sinatras took cover, and began firing back.

But Trevor's weapon was the only one that did not contain a silencer. Carly heard the gunfire as soon as he began firing, and she quickly woke up and lifted up in bed. When Trevor saw her, and saw that she was at risk for harm, his heart slammed against his chest. "*Nooo!*" he cried and jumped over the nightstand, diving onto Carly and knocking her back down onto the bed. But as he did, Mick took a shot that landed, and Trevor crashed down like dead weight on top of Carly.

When they didn't hear anymore gunfire from in front of them or behind them, Mick and Charles stood erect. But then they heard a different sound. The sound of a woman crying. Mick looked at Charles, and Charles, with Mick covering him, hurried to the bed. When he moved Trevor's lifeless body aside, he realized somebody with the voice of a woman was beneath him. Charles quickly turned on the nightstand lamp. When he saw that it was Carly lying in that bed, crying, his heart fell through his shoe. He had no idea she had come to Boston!

When Carly looked up and saw that her

father was standing there, she was shocked too. But for a different reason. She was terrified for Trevor.

"You killed him!" she cried. *"You killed him!"*

Charles and Mick had taken Carly from the Reese estate, kicking and screaming, as they got away before Trevor's front gate men, not to mention the Boston police, could surround them. But as Mick drove to the Boston airstrip, with Charles in the backseat with Carly in case she tried to make a run for it, they were worried. The kind of security they encountered at Reese's home was more than Mafia. No mobster needed that many levels of security where there were men on guard in the basement too. Was he Fed undercover? Was he Fed outright?

"Have you ever seen anything like it?" Charles asked.

"No," Mick admitted. "Not quite that vast."

"Who is this guy?" Charles asked. "What's going on with him?"

"Nothing is going on with him," Carly said angrily. "You broke into his home. You fired on him. You killed him!" Tears reappeared in her eyes.

"He was firing on us," Charles said. "He was no saint, Carly."

"Neither are you," Carly said. "Or Uncle Mick." Then she thought about what she had done to Ethan Campbell. "Or *me*!" she blared.

"You didn't know the whole story," Charles said. "You didn't know what he was up to."

Carly looked at her father. "What was he up to? You don't know either!"

"I know," Mick said, "that he has a vendetta against me."

"Why?" Carly asked.

Mick hesitated, but he knew she deserved the truth. "I killed his father," he said.

Carly's heart dropped. "What?" she asked.

"He probably hired you," Mick continued, "as what we call in my world a *just in case*."

But Carly was shaking her head. "Trevor isn't like that. *Wasn't* like that," she corrected herself, and her tears returned.

"You don't know what he was like," Charles said. "What are you talking about?"

"I'm talking about Trevor. I'm talking about the man I knew."

"That man wanted to kill your uncle, Carly!" Charles yelled.

"My uncle killed his father, Dad!" Carly yelled back. "What's the damn difference?"

Charles saw a hard edge to Carly he had

never seen before. Even Mick looked through the rearview at her. Was this change all because of Trevor Reese? Or was it deeper than that, and a long time coming? Was Carly, her father wondered, finally coming out of her protective shell?

A cell phone began to ring. Carly knew it was her dial tone, but she didn't even think she had her purse. But while Charles put clothes on Carly back at Reese's house, Mick found her purse when he double checked the room to make sure they were leaving no evidence behind. It was lying on the passenger seat beside him now. He picked it up and tossed it to Carly. "It's yours," he said.

Carly didn't want to be bothered, but she reached into her purse, pulled out her cell phone, and answered. "Yes?"

"Carly," a voice, a very faint but familiar voice, said.

Carly's heart began to pound. "Trevor?" she asked.

Mick almost wrecked the car when he heard that name. He looked through the rearview at her. Charles was already staring at her.

"You're alive?" Carly asked excitedly.

But Trevor's faint voice had a question of his own. "Are you okay?"

"Yes!" Carly said, with joy in her voice.

"Are you safe?"

"I'm with my father. Yes," she said.

"Good," he said. "Good."

"Where are you?" Carly asked.

"On my way to Baptist," Trevor said. Baptist, Carly knew, was a hospital in town.

"Are you okay?" Trevor asked her again.

"I'm fine," she said. "I'm with my father. I'm safe."

"Good," he said again. And then the call went dead.

"Trevor?" Carly said into the phone. "Trevor?" She was panicking now. "Oh my God. Please, *Trevor*!"

Charles removed the phone from her hand and checked it. "He hung up, babe," he said.

Carly looked at her father. "Turn the car around," she said. "Turn the car around!"

"Don't talk crazy, Carly," Charles said. "We're heading for Uncle Mick's plane and getting the hell out of this town."

"Not with me you aren't," Carly said firmly. "You either turn this car around, or I'll get out and walk to that hospital."

"It could be a set up," Mick said, although he suspected that it wasn't.

"It's no setup," Carly said. "He's alive, and I have to see him!"

Charles knew he had to stop sugarcoating this situation with his daughter. "Trevor Reese is most likely a mob boss, Carly," he said.

"You mean like Uncle Mick?" Carly asked.

Mick smiled.

"Or worse," Charles said. "He could be a federal agent undercover. Under deep cover as a mobster."

Carly gave herself a chance to compose herself. She looked at her father. "I know I'm acting irrationally, Dad," she said. "I know I'm not behaving in my normal way. But when I decided to leave Jericho earlier today, I decided because I was tired." Her voice broke when she said that word. Mick looked through his rearview.

"Tired of what?" Charles asked her.

"Tired of going through life without living. Tired of never taking any risks. Tired of living the way other people want me to live. I'm tired, Dad."

Charles's heart swelled with pain. "But sweetheart," he said, "this man isn't the antidote to your need to live. He's the poison. You won't be taking a risk on love if you hook up with him. You'll be taking a risk with your life."

Carly held firm. "But if it isn't much of a life anyway, just an existence, it's a risk worth taking. What do I have to lose?"

Charles felt torn. He didn't know what to do. He couldn't hand his baby over to a man who very well might be using her to get to Mick. But as with many things in his life, the question answered itself when Mick's cell phone began to ring.

Mick pulled it out and answered it as he drove. He wasn't accustomed to being the driver of the group, but he knew Charles had the most influence of any man alive over Carly. "This is Sinatra," he said.

As Mick listened to his phone call, Carly listened to her heart. And she was being told, as clear as crystal, that her heart belonged with Trevor. They were in early days still. She understood that. And he very well might not want her like that. But he saved her life. He took a bullet to save her life. And even as he fought for his own life, he phoned to make sure she was okay. He might be everything and more that her father and uncle declared that he was, and she understood that. But she saw him as her chance to live. She saw him as her chance to dare to do what she wanted to do for a change. She saw him as a man she could grow to love deeply.

When Mick ended the call, he seemed perplexed. Even Carly saw it. Charles saw it especially. "What's wrong?" he asked.

Mick exhaled. "It's not him," he said.

Charles frowned. "It's not who?"

"Trevor Reese."

"What about Trevor?" Carly asked.

"That was one of my men," Mick said. "He said there had been a mistake."

"What kind of mistake?" Charles asked.

"When I ordered them to crosscheck any of the men I had to take out, and to crosscheck them with the name Reese, they did that. When they saw Reese, they assumed that was the guy. But it was James Reese, not Trevor Reese."

Charles frowned. Carly didn't understand either. "What do you mean?" Charles asked. "Make it plain, Mick."

"The guy I iced," Mick said, "wasn't Trevor's father. There's no connection. I have no connection with Trevor Reese. At least, not *that* connection."

Carly was ecstatic. Charles was still confused. "Then why did he want that woman to spy on my family?" he asked.

Mick said three words he hated to say. "I don't know," he said.

And as the car pulled into the airstrip where Mick's private plane was waiting, Charles didn't know either. But he knew he had a decision to make. He stared at his daughter. This was crazy on every level. How could he even think it? But somehow he knew he had to let her go. She was a grown woman. She had to live her life for herself. He had to allow her that opportunity.

Mick knew it too. That was why, when he stopped the car, he handed the keys to Charles. Charles handed the keys to Carly.

"Live your life," Charles said to his beloved daughter. "But when you find that it's too much for you to handle alone, you'd better call me."

"And me," Mick added.

Carly smiled. And hugged her father. "You know I will," she said.

But they weren't that trusting. Mick ordered the group of men he had waiting in an SUV at the airstrip in case he needed to call in backup, to follow her to that hospital. "Blanket her," he ordered. And they took off too.

But what faced Mick and Charles weren't so cut and dry. When they thought it was a past connection, it was easier to swallow. But now they didn't even have that to hang their hats upon. All they knew was that Trevor Reese was up to something, and it involved the Sinatra family. What they didn't know, and this was a big lack of knowledge, was what that something was.

"We'll find out," Mick reassured his brother. "I can promise you that."

"And they got the name wrong?" Charles asked, still astounded by this turn of events.

Mick nodded with a flash of anger in his eyes. "Yup."

"That's some incompetent shit there," Charles said.

"I know," Mick acknowledged.

Charles gave him a hard look. "But it's not worth killing anybody over. They messed up. That's all."

"Their fuck up almost cost us our lives," Mick reminded him. "Their fuck up almost cost Carly hers too. That failure will not go unpunished."

Charles hated to hear about more carnage. But he understood. Mick's very survival depended on his strength. He touched his younger brother on the arm, as they headed for the plane.

By the time Carly made it to the hospital, Trevor was in the emergency room, surrounded by heavy guard. When she saw him, her heart leaped with joy and she hurried toward him. But his guards stopped her.

"Trevor!" she cried. "He wants to see me,"

she said, although she wasn't certain of that. "Trevor!"

When Trevor heard her voice over all of the noises around him, his heart went still. Was he delusional? But he heard it again. *"Trevor,"* he heard. And he was certain now.

He looked in the direction of the sound, and saw Carly attempting to go around his guards. "Let her through!" he ordered in a voice so faint his men didn't hear him. "Let her through!" he said again, and they heard it that time.

The men stepped aside, and Carly ran to Trevor.

Trevor was in tremendous pain, and was already hooked up to an I-V, but he still had enough strength within him to pull Carly into his arms. "Carly," he said. "Carly."

He couldn't say anymore, but that was enough. Because Carly had already made up her mind. She was ready to sink or swim, ride or die, with Trevor. And it felt as impulsive and spontaneous and reckless as she wanted it to feel. It felt strange and different. Messy for once. Like life.

EPILOGUE

They sat in the family room and watched the election night returns in a kind of resigned silence. Charles, with his arm around Jenay and with his youngest child on his lap, sat on the sofa. Brent and Makayla, hand in hand, sat beside them. The floor was littered with everybody else: Tony, with Sharon Flannigan sitting beside him. Robert, with his young nephew, Junior, sitting beside him. And Donald and Ashley sitting beside each other. But as they all watched the big screen TV with rapt attention, the writing was already on the wall.

"It's going to be Cruikshank," Tony said. "There's no way the mayor can overtake that big a lead."

Donald looked at their father. "What does it mean, Dad?" he asked.

"It means," Robert interjected, "that Brent and Makayla are going to be fired from their jobs. Cruikshank has been promising it since he first started running all those months ago. That's one campaign promise I'll bet you he'll keep. That's what it means."

"It means more than that," Tony said. "Cruikshank promised to bring Dad down too."

Everybody looked at their father, as if they had forgotten about that fact. But Donald wasn't believing it any way. He smiled. "Go on," he said. "He can't bring Dad down."

"For real," Ashley agreed.

"For wrong," Tony disagreed. "He'll be mayor. He can pass all kinds of ordinances. He can do whatever he wants."

"So what does this all mean, Dad?" Donald asked again, and everybody looked at Charles.

"It means we fight," Charles said, "to hold onto what's ours."

"Damn right," Brent said.

"What are you talking about?" Donald asked Brent. "Cruikshank's going to fire you and your wife."

"Really, Daddy?" Junior asked his father.

"No, son," Brent responded.

"What do you mean no?" Donald asked.

"I mean if the vote tally holds and Cruikshank is nominated mayor of Jericho, he won't have to fire me. I will resign," Brent said.

"As will I," Makayla said. "Although it's doubtful that my position could be placed under his jurisdiction anyway, despite that city council vote."

"But why not fight for your jobs?" Ashley

asked. "Dad said we should fight."

"But that'll be the wrong fight," Brent said. "Dad is going to need all hands on deck. Me, Makayla, all of us."

Jenay smiled. She and Charles loved it when Brent took control. "That's right," Jenay said. "The Sinatra Corporation is a family business. Brent and Makayla has agreed to come to work in that business. Cruikshank's election could be a blessing in disguise."

"Wow," Robert said. "So that means all of us will be working for Dad."

"That's right," Jenay said proudly.

"All except Carly," Ashley reminded them.

"But that's where you're wrong," a voice said, and everybody looked toward the entrance into the family room. Carly was standing at the entrance.

"Look at you!" Ashley said. "All decked down in designer everything. You go girl. You don't look like a book worm anymore!"

"You look great, Carly," Robert agreed.

"Thanks," Carly said with a smile as she made her way toward her family.

"What do you mean Ash was wrong?" Tony asked her.

"Hey, former boss," Carly said to Sharon as she walked closer.

Sharon smiled. "I was your boss for about

two minutes," she said. "We still miss you at Saint Cat's."

Carly smiled. "Thanks."

"We would love to have you back," Sharon said. "Would you like to come back?"

"No ma'am," Carly said quickly and Carly, along with everybody else, laughed. Her family had never seen her so vivacious.

"What I meant," Carly said to Tony, "when I said you were wrong, is that I'm the only PR professional in this family. To beat back Cruikshank and his plans to take Dad down will require a lot of cutting edge public relations. I'll help out every way I can."

Charles pulled Jenay closer. They were pleased to hear it.

"What about your gangster boyfriend?" Donald asked. "Is it over already? I told you it wasn't going to last. It's over, isn't it?"

Carly smiled. "Not hardly," she said. "It's just getting started. Trust."

Her siblings laughed, and her parents looked at each other. They still had serious issues with Trevor Reese. There was just too much mystery surrounding him and not enough information for them to make any factual conclusions. But Carly's happiness could not be denied. Even Charles could see her glow.

And as she joined them in the family room, sitting on the floor with her other siblings, Charles also could not deny the challenge. Things were changing dramatically for all of them, and it was going to take a full court press to beat back every challenge. But as Charles pulled Jenay tighter into his arms, he knew that they, as a couple and as a family, were going to get through this just fine.

Visit www.mallorymonroebooks.com
for more information on all of her titles.

ABOUT THE AUTHOR

Mallory Monroe is the bestselling author of numerous books. Visit www.mallorymonroebooks.com for more information on all of her titles.